On Stage, Please

On Stage, Please

a story by
Veronica Tennant

illustrations by Rita Briansky

Holt, Rinehart and Winston
New York

First published in Canada by McClelland and Stewart Limited
under the same title. First American edition published in
1979 by Holt, Rinehart and Winston.
Copyright © 1977 by McClelland and Stewart Limited
Copyright © 1979 by Holt, Rinehart and Winston
All rights reserved, including the right to reproduce
this book or portions thereof in any form.
Printed in the United States of America
10 9 8 7 6 5 4 3 2 1

Library of Congress Cataloging in Publication Data

Tennant, Veronica.   On stage, please.

SUMMARY: A young girl begins serious training
for a career as a professional dancer.
{1. Ballet dancing—Fiction}   I. Briansky,
Rita. II. Title. PZ7.T26390n 1979 [Fic]   79-4819
ISBN 0-03-049306-4

to John

On Stage, Please

Part I

Chapter One

"Come quick," Jim and Susan shouted, grabbing Jennifer and pulling her over to the rail of the ship's upper deck. Mr. and Mrs. Allen were right behind them in the growing rush of passengers. "Look! Montreal!" Sue cried.

Jennifer hung on tightly to her red plaid bag while taking in deep breaths of fresh air. Canada at last! After six days at sea she gazed silently at more snow than she had seen in all the nine years of her life. "And we've still hundreds of miles to go," Mr. Allen said. "It's going to take us a little while to get used to the vast distances in this country."

Jennifer recalled her father's words when he had made the decision to leave England and accept the new job. "Just think of the possibilities! This will be a new life for us!" His enthusiasm had almost convinced Jennifer that she would not be lonely or miss the friends in London she was leaving behind. Now the nagging questions swarmed back into her mind, especially the one she dared not ask. Was Canada really the place where she, Jennifer Allen, could make her dream come true?

As they lined up to go through Customs Jennifer heard people around her speaking in French. Some of the people in Sault Ste. Marie, where they were going to live, spoke French and Jennifer wanted to learn it as fast as she could. "*Merci*" and "*bonjour*" were two words she knew already and she practiced them soundlessly now, liking the way they rolled off her tongue. Still, if the Customs man spoke to her she wouldn't be able to understand him. And she was bothered by the thought that he might want to look inside her red plaid bag. She fingered the key in her pocket to make sure it was still there.

The officer studied their passports and immigration papers. "And where are you going to live?" he asked Jennifer with a smile, and in English. "Solt St. Mary," she answered promptly, proud that he'd asked her. Her mother and father laughed. "How many times do I have to tell you?" Sue said. "It's Su-e-OOOO Ste. Marie!!"

They were met at the docks by a driver who had been sent from Mr. Allen's company. A good while later, the movers had loaded the truck that would be following with their belongings, the Allens had piled into the driver's station wagon, and they were speeding along what seemed like an endless stretch of road. Jennifer, seated between Jim and Susan, kept fidgeting in an attempt to look out the window. Very little that she managed to see resembled the pictures in the glossy pamphlets that her father had shown her.

Their journey dragged on with never a break in the blur of trees or the drone of the engine. Everyone had fallen silent. Jennifer, resisting sleep, pulled the red bag on her lap, slipped the key from her pocket, and unlocked it. She rearranged inside the new black leotard and the stiff pair of pink leather slippers that had cost her several weeks of allowance. Then she took out the crinkled program that was the beginning of everything. It was from *Cinderella*, the first ballet performance that Jennifer had seen. It would not be the last, for Jennifer was going to become a dancer. Nothing was more certain in her mind than that.

Smoothing the worn paper, Jennifer studied each page as though she were looking at it for the first time. She sighed, remembering that wonderful night with her mother at the Grand Opera House in London. She closed her eyes, picturing herself in the red velvet dress. She could almost see it all. . . .

"Ohhhh!" Jennifer had exclaimed when the usher directed them to their front-row seats in the first balcony. By leaning over the railing slightly she was able to see right into the orchestra pit. What a din the musicians made tuning their instruments! Jennifer had counted the players—seventy-five—and each one busy practicing his or her own part in the score. Then the first violinist tapped his bow against the music stand and as though by magic, the individual instruments came together as one. "They are sounding the note A to make certain they are well tuned," her mother had said.

Gradually the lights dimmed until the great hall was lost in blackness. The stillness was broken by spatters of applause as the conductor, his stick in his hand, entered the orchestra pit. The audience watched as he took his position on the podium and the musicians fixed their eyes upon him as he raised his arms.

Music filled the air and the curtain rose on Cinderella sweeping mountains of ashes under an immense stone fireplace. No words were spoken, yet it was clear what the girl in rags was saying as she guided her broom through a dance of sorrow.

Shrill, discordant notes warned of the entrance of the stepsisters and in they marched, one tall, the other small, grotesque with their powdered wigs and painted faces. Their antics were comical as they squabbled, tripping over their own feet and finery. Then they turned their wrath upon Cinderella. Darting, poking, jumping, they attacked her with unreasonable fury and Jennifer remembered how she had squirmed in her seat when the ugly stepmother dove in to help them out. As she thought about it now, she couldn't get over the thrill of seeing her favorite story come to life. The way the dancers moved seemed to tell the tale more clearly than any words could.

When the fairy godmother appeared, it was magic! The kitchen miraculously disappeared and an enchanted land became visible as thirty fairy-like forms spun and swept across the stage. Jennifer's eyes had filled with wonder, for the power and grace of these dancers expressed what she had found only in dreams.

Cinderella was the most beautiful of them all. It was

not just the prettiness of her face that made her so; it was the way she tilted her head to show sorrow and used her feet to indicate shyness, and the way she moved her whole body when she wished to express love and joy.

Jennifer dreamed on, remembering the ball where the handsome prince danced so spectacularly and gasps of admiration rippled through the audience. Then, when he and Cinderella met, the music swept them into their dance for two. This "pas de deux" had been the highlight of the performance, with soaring lifts and gliding runs and tender moments of quiet.

"Bravo! Bravo! Bravo!" the audience cried when it was over. Jennifer had been unable to move. She could not accept the fact that the music had ceased and the curtain had fallen. Then her inner excitement had found its way to her hands. She clapped until her fingers were sore and tingling, and she too leapt to her feet calling "Bravo!" as loudly as she could.

The voices in the front of the car started up again, and Jennifer remembered with a shiver where she was. As she listened to her parents question the driver about Canada she was struck by how different their accent was from his.

"Are the children still asleep?" she heard her father ask.

"Yes," her mother said. "By the way, we'll be looking for a ballet school in Sault Ste. Marie," she added softly. Jennifer sat up. Her mother continued, "Our youngest is the right age to begin and she's been dreaming about lessons ever since we went to a performance last year."

"Ah," the man replied, "my niece used to take dancing but she didn't seem to enjoy it too well. What was the

19

name?" He scratched his head. "Oh yes, Vincent, Mr. Vincent. He's supposed to be good, he must be—he's always advertising in the newspaper."

Jennifer quietly returned her treasures to the red plaid bag, then settled back. She smiled as she drifted into sleep. Canada might turn out all right after all. She was going to learn how to really dance! She was going to be beautiful, just like Cinderella.

* * *

When she felt the motor switch off Jennifer sprang wide awake. "Well, here you are, home at last," the driver announced, stretching from behind the wheel. "It's been a long haul for you folks."

Rubbing her eyes, Jennifer peered out the window. They were parked in front of a yellow brick house with dark green shutters. Jim hopped out to wave down the truck that had been following them and Jennifer jumped out after him and looked around. She saw groups of children dressed in colorful snowsuits collecting along the driveway. They spoke to each other in French. Some of them had snowballs in their hands. Jennifer was afraid of their stares until she caught the warm smile of a girl with curly black hair, who reminded her of her friend Kate in London.

As boxes started accumulating on the street, some of the older children dug a path through the snow to the house. Soon a long line of helpers staggered in and out. "Come and see the house," Mrs. Allen called from within. Jennifer ran inside. She found her mother in a bedroom upstairs. "This one will probably be yours, Jenny," she said. Jennifer hugged her in delight. She had always wanted a room of her own. She looked out the window and could not withhold a shout of excitement; in the garden were scrambles of snow-blanketed bushes and a great gnarled tree with a swing.

By late evening every room in the house was cluttered and confusion reigned: Jennifer's mother couldn't locate the tea; Jim spent an hour searching for the towels after his shower; Sue couldn't find her radio; and Jennifer burrowed through mountains of clothes looking for her nightgown.

But in a few days things settled down and once their own furniture and pictures were arranged, the house even began to feel familiar. Sooner than they would have liked, Jim and Susan were enrolled in the junior high school and Jennifer was put into grade four in the public school around the corner.

Chapter Two

*E*ach day when Jennifer came home from school and joined her family around the dinner table, she hoped there would be news for her. It was now two weeks since they had arrived in Canada and everyone seemed to be adjusting. Jim talked incessantly about hockey, and Sue had made several friends. But so far, no one had said a word to Jennifer about the ballet lessons.

"What are you brooding about?" Jim asked one evening.

"I'm not brooding," Jennifer replied haughtily.

"I know what Jenny's thinking about," her mother said quietly. "In a day or two everything will be arranged."

* * *

On Saturday morning Jennifer awoke very early. The hours seemed to drag until eleven o'clock when they

would leave the house. She had opened and shut her red plaid bag a dozen times. It now contained a hair brush, the large pins her mother had bought her so she could fasten her hair in a bun, white socks, and of course the black leotard and pink leather slippers.

The ballet studio was downtown, in a part of the city that Jennifer had not yet visited. As she and her mother rode in the bus, Jennifer kept her face glued to the window, taking in all the strange and wonderful sights. "Remember the way, Jenny," her mother said, "so that next time you can go on your own." Jennifer read every sign at every corner, anxiously watching for Spring Street where the ballet school was located.

"There it is!" she called suddenly.

As soon as they were off the bus Jennifer ran down the street looking for number 397-C which was the address of Mr. Vincent's studio.

"Wait, Jennifer," her mother kept calling. "I can't keep up with you."

When they reached number 397, all they saw was a book and record store. Jennifer looked up at her mother in alarm. "Don't worry," Mrs. Allen said after a pause, "it's upstairs," and she pointed to a sign beside the door: "GUSTAVO VINCENT, TEACHER OF GRAND CLASSICAL BALLET – THREE FLIGHTS UP.

The moment they opened the door they heard the tinkling of a piano and the thumping of feet. As they climbed the narrow stairs Jennifer heard a man bellowing, "Up! Down! Hold! Hold! Down! Up! Hold! Hold!" then, "No, Barbara, no!"

By the time they reached the top of the stairs Jennifer

felt very sorry for Barbara. While her mother registered her at the desk, she was led down a curved hallway to the girls' dressing room to get changed. She had put her long hair into a ponytail but now she noticed that all the other girls had their hair in fancy buns with ribbons on top. Jennifer tried to twist her hair into a knot and stuck as many pins in as she could, but the bun kept wobbling about every time she moved her head. Out of the bag came her leotard, her white socks and pink slippers. Some of the other girls were pulling on pink tights just like professional dancers. How Jennifer wished she could wear those instead of showing her bare legs above the white socks.

At noon Jennifer followed about ten girls and four boys into the ballet studio. A class had just ended and the air was hot and sticky with the dancers' sweat. The students leaving the room looked exhausted. One girl with a blotchy red face looked as though she had been crying. That must be Barbara, Jennifer thought.

"Are you the new girl?" a voice boomed out at Jennifer.

She nodded nervously, and she was surprised to see that the big voice came from a little man with a shiny bald head and a very red nose.

"You're," he consulted a piece of paper, "Jennifer Allen?"

"Yes," she squeaked.

Was this Mr. Vincent? He was not at all the way she had imagined him. He wore a white T-shirt over his

25

protruding tummy, shiny black tights and white sneakers. Without another word, he padded out of the room, fumbling with his cigar.

"Come and stand behind me at the barre," Jennifer heard a whisper. "Class won't be starting for a couple of minutes till he's had his smoke." The girl who spoke to Jennifer was very pretty. She was wearing pink tights. "My name's Shirley. I've been taking lessons for a year. Don't worry about him, he's just an old fool." Jennifer looked around uneasily but Mr. Vincent was still puffing away outside.

The room in which she stood was enormous, with two rows of wooden bars attached to three of the walls. The fourth wall was entirely mirrored. In the centre of it was a carpeted raised platform with a chair on top. That must be where Mr. Vincent sits, thought Jennifer. In two of the corners she noticed flat wooden boxes containing mounds of fine, yellow powder. Some of the older students were walking over and energetically grinding their ballet slippers in the dust. "That's resin," explained Shirley when she saw Jennifer's puzzled expression. "We use it so that we won't slip on the floor."

In the corner near the teacher's chair was a grand piano beside which there sat a lady with wavy white hair piled high on her head. Jennifer could not rid herself of the feeling that the woman was watching her so she smiled shyly, but the pianist raised a finger furtively to her lips. Instantly everyone stopped talking. Mr. Vincent had entered the room.

"Okay, okay, okay. Let's get on with it," he bellowed. "Exercise Number One in all five positions."

At this command the pianist plinked at her keys and the students followed her tune with a series of knee bends.

Jennifer had expected Mr. Vincent to explain things to her. What did he mean by the five positions? She reached up to the lower rung of the barre beside her and awkwardly tried to copy Shirley standing in front.

"*Thwack!*" Jennifer felt a stinging slap across the back of her knees. "Don't you know how to stand in first position?" Mr. Vincent had come up from behind. Before she could explain that this was her first lesson, he had prodded both her heels into a straight line. Jennifer's knees jabbed like knives; she was rocking backwards and forwards. She clung to the barre for support. "There," he said, aligning her feet. But the second he let go, her toes sprang back to pointing forwards. "No! No!" Mr. Vincent pounced, forcing them sideways again. "Hold it!" Jennifer was unable to sustain the position by herself and the teacher walked away from her in disgust.

Dismayed, she tried to continue with the class. Each exercise became faster and more complicated. Her eyes never left Shirley working in front, but it was no use. Jennifer simply couldn't make her body do the same things. At one point, while attempting fifth position, one foot knocked the other out from under her and she found herself on the floor. Mr. Vincent saw this and marched over. Oh, good, thought Jennifer, standing up flustered, maybe now he'll show me how. But he stood waving his cigar in her face and screaming so loudly that she couldn't hear what he was saying. He smacked her

27

arms, telling her to relax, and then he poked her in the stomach. "Don't fall," he grunted. There were snickers in the room. Mr. Vincent heard them. "Don't fall," he repeated looking around, quite pleased with himself.

I mustn't cry, Jennifer vowed as she hung on. She blinked her eyes hard to keep the tears from forming. As the lesson became more and more unbearable, she prayed for it to finish. Her eyes fastened on the minute hand of the clock. Oh, please, please make it soon, she silently implored.

At last the hour was up and Mr. Vincent dismissed the class. Jennifer ran from the room. She hastily changed her clothes, not listening to Shirley's words. "Cheer up, we all went through this. You'll learn."

During the bus ride home Jennifer was very quiet. Again she kept her face pressed to the window but this time it was so that her mother wouldn't see the tears that were slipping down her face. Why did Mr. Vincent pick on me like that? she wondered. Didn't he think I was good enough to be a dancer? But he didn't even give me a chance! She dabbed at her eyes with her coat sleeves. If only she could prove to him that he'd made a mistake.

* * *

The following Saturday at eleven o'clock Jennifer set off for the studio again, this time on her own.

"Are you sure you'll be all right?" her mother asked worriedly.

"I'm fine," Jennifer insisted. "There are exactly eleven stops to Spring Street."

If anything, Jennifer's second ballet lesson was more

miserable than the first. All week she had prepared herself for being yelled at, but now Mr. Vincent ignored her altogether. As she struggled into first position, he walked right up as if to say something to her but then he. gave Shirley a niggling correction.

"Forward and back bends next," he called out and he snapped his fingers driving the pianist to play the music faster.

Determined as she was, Jennifer failed to keep in time. Her back muscles ached and soon she was gasping for breath. She tried to catch Mr. Vincent's eye to show him how hard she was working but it was useless. Not from anyone in the room could she find reassurance. She noticed the other students, even Shirley, looking just as strained and miserable as she felt. It was hot and the ballet studio smelled of cigar smoke and sweat. In desperation Jennifer contemplated escaping when Mr. Vincent's back was turned. But he never stayed still for very long and though he refused to correct her she felt that he was watching her. His voice never stopped barking commands. "Face the barre. Now, sixty-four jumps in first and second position." He rapped the piano, indicating his desired tempo. "And-er-one, and-er-two . . ." There was no sound. The pianist's yellowed hands remained immobile in her lap while she stared fixedly at Mr. Vincent.

"And-er-one, and-er-two," he repeated, glowering.

"It's time to stop," the old lady said. And looking at the clock on the wall Jennifer saw that indeed it was. She held her breath as Mr. Vincent turned beet red, but then he shrugged his shoulders and walked out of the room.

When Jennifer returned home that night she was again very quiet about her ballet lesson.

"Well, how's it going?" asked her father. But when he saw his daughter's sorrowful look he didn't press for an answer.

Shame made Jennifer even more wretched. She suspected that her parents really could not afford the added expense of the ballet lessons. After dreaming about ballet for so long, how could she now admit to such disappointment?

* * *

A few days later Jennifer was sitting in her room by the open window when she overheard her mother talking to Madame Beauchamp across the fence. "But why didn't you say so?" the neighbour exclaimed. "You should never have taken her to Mr. Vincent. He takes young children and cripples them. Do you know how dangerous it is to learn ballet from a bad teacher?"

"Why, well, no . . . "

Jennifer couldn't catch her mother's stammered reply but now Madame Beauchamp's voice grew angrier. "The children's bones are soft. They have not been fully formed. He overdevelops their muscles. He forces girls up on their toes before they are strong enough and this can cause terrible damage." Madame Beauchamp was yelling now. "Sault Ste. Marie has quite a few fine ballet schools but this Gustavo Vincent is a charlatan!"

That night Mrs. Allen spoke to Jennifer. "Mrs. Beauchamp knows about these things because her daughter, Danièlle, has studied ballet seriously for many years. She's seventeen and a student at the Professional School of Ballet in Toronto. She's coming home for the long weekend and Madame Beauchamp suggested that she talk to you herself. So thank goodness you only had two lessons with that terrible Mr. Vincent, and . . . ''

Jennifer clung to her mother and sobbed as if her heart would break.

Chapter Three

Something about Danièlle Beauchamp made people guess she was a ballet dancer. She moved in a special way; she even walked with an air of delicate grace. She had a tiny face with features that were perfectly moulded and her eyes were wide and grey. Her dark chestnut hair was drawn back and coiled in thick braids at the top of her head. From the moment Jennifer met Danièlle, she began to idolize her. All that weekend Jennifer hardly left her side. She asked a thousand questions about what it was really like to study ballet.

"Contrary to what Mr. Vincent may think, you start slowly," explained Danièlle. "It takes many years for the turn-out of your hips to form. It will take at least two years, maybe more, of careful training before you'll be allowed up on your toes – remember, we use the French word *pointes* – and even then you won't be dancing on them away from the barre. There'll be exercises and more exercises until your toes and your arches, your ankles and your calves, your knees and your thighs, are strong enough to hold you up."

"You mean," said Jennifer, "it could take years before I'm able to dance like you?"

"Of course," Danièlle replied. "It's a gradual building process. And for the rest of your life, even after you've become a dancer, you'll have to work on all those exercises. And don't forget your arms. They must be trained to look as soft as a floating cloud. There's no part of your body that you won't use. At ballet school you can get corrections for the baby finger, even the angle of the head."

Jennifer thought back to that evening at the opera house in London and she remembered Cinderella expressing sorrow and joy with her body instead of with words. "That's what I want most in the world," said Jennifer dreamily, "to be a ballet dancer."

"It's not all glamour, you know," Danièlle said sharply. "Are you prepared to work day after day, hour after hour?"

Jennifer's eyes shone as she looked up at Danièlle. "Yes, I am. I want to go to your school and learn everything."

"Do you know how many girls and boys try to get into the Professional School? There are hundreds from all across Canada and the world. Out of every audition they accept one or two. It's not enough that you want to be a dancer. You need the right body, intelligence and talent."

Now Danièlle looked down at the little girl and spoke more gently. "But, Jennifer, would you really want to leave your parents and sister and brother and go live in a strange city by yourself? Toronto is very different from Sault Ste. Marie. It's a big place and awfully far away."

Jennifer hadn't thought about that and she began to feel confused.

"It's a difficult decision, believe me, I had to make it too," said Danièlle. She put her arm around Jennifer who by now had grown quite glum. "How old are you, anyway?"

"I'm nine," said Jennifer.

"Oh, well, that settles it," said Danièlle. "The school won't take students from outside Toronto before they're ten."

Jennifer was almost relieved to hear this. It was all so much more complicated than she had imagined. After all, she loved her mother and father, and Susan and Jim, and she wasn't at all sure she could go away and leave them. Besides, what chance did she have of getting into the Professional School? Could she be the one in a hundred that they accepted? Not if Mr. Vincent was the judge! But then Danièlle had told her that you didn't even have to know how to dance when you went for the audition. Somehow the examiners could tell from the shape of your body and alertness of your mind whether you could be trained to be a ballet dancer. It all sounds very frightening, thought Jennifer. I'm going to have to think a great deal about this. Maybe in a year when I'm ten things will be different.

Chapter Four

*J*ennifer's new life in Canada had its ups and downs. There were times when she could not imagine living anywhere else. But then there were nights when in her dreams she poured out her heart to the friends she had left behind in London.

She tried her best in grade four; her marks in English and French were good and she worked very hard to catch up in history, but when it came to math. she slid to the bottom of her class. She often left those lessons in tears, having failed to wring logic from her muddled mind. No matter how carefully the teacher explained the problems to her, Jennifer could never figure them out. If it hadn't been for Anna, the curly-haired girl who lived next door to Jennifer, it would have been altogether hopeless. Anna reminded her so much of her friend Kate in London and they had become good friends very soon after Jennifer moved to Sault Ste. Marie. Anna, who was French, explained so many things about Canada to Jennifer, and when the other children made fun of her British accent and different clothes, Anna defended her. "How would you like to be treated if you were in a new country?" she asked them, standing defiantly with her hands on her hips.

What bothered Jennifer was the suspicion that even if she had been born in Sault Ste. Marie she would still have been different. Sometimes she could be just as lively and noisy as the other children, but there were other times when she would suddenly become shy, almost sad. Only Anna understood Jennifer's need to retreat into a world of her own and she never seemed to notice when Jennifer would disappear. Anna knew that most of the time Jennifer was at the back of her garden in the one area she had begged her parents not to tidy up. She had her own little spot there amid a scramble of bushes hidden away from the rest of the world. And though Danièlle Beauchamp's words of warning – "It's not all glamour" – echoed in her ears, Jennifer could not forget her dream no matter how hard she tried.

Very soon after they arrived in Canada, Jennifer asked her parents for a pair of skates. The sight of the other children skimming over the ice filled her with a longing to join them. How dismayed Jennifer was to find herself clinging to the boards, terrified to let go, inching her way around the rink. Each day Anna would guide her protesting friend away from the supporting rails. Jennifer's ankles wobbled and rolled as if her bones were made of rubber and she tumbled many times

on the cold and bruising ice. Still, she persevered and by her second Canadian winter Jennifer found herself skating with growing confidence. She often imagined that she were dancing as she glided in graceful, looping circles.

One day while she was skating alone and lost in her own world, she suddenly became aware of laughter and noticed a group of children pointing at her. Jennifer turned crimson. What unusual movements had she made while she was so deep in her dream?

"She's weird," Jennifer heard a girl say to the others in her group.

Tears stung her eyes, and trying to blink them away she went over to the bench and sat down. She kept her eyes riveted to her skates, painfully aware that the children were still staring at her. Then suddenly there stood a boy before her, an older boy who must have been about seventeen or eighteen.

"Don't feel badly," he said to Jennifer. "Those kids just don't understand and that's what makes them mean. Tell me, are you in training to be a ballet dancer?"

Jennifer looked into the boy's eyes in amazement. "How did you guess?" she asked, but her voice was so soft he could hardly hear it.

The boy sat down on the bench and spoke to Jennifer as if she were his own age. He told her how much he loved ballet, how he had seen many thrilling performances and wanted to study himself.

"My family were strongly opposed," he said, "so I stayed with sports instead. But I know I'll regret it for the rest of my life." Jennifer nodded, thinking how sad if his parents had thought ballet was just for girls. He explained that he was now eighteen and it was too late to start professional training. "How old are you?" he asked Jennifer.

"I'll be ten in a month's time."

"Well then, you're the perfect age to begin. Take my advice and don't let anything stop you."

That night, for the first time in many months, Jennifer again brought up the subject of the ballet school. Apparently she was not the only one who had been thinking of it because her parents did not seem surprised.

"But you know, Jennifer," her father said, "you could be very disappointed. You heard how difficult it is to get into the Professional School of Ballet. And I must admit, I do worry about what it would cost us to send you to Toronto."

Jennifer's mother tried to talk her into just taking lessons in Sault Ste. Marie. "Mr. Vincent is hardly the only ballet teacher here," she reminded Jennifer. "Mrs. Beauchamp has recommended at least two others. We could go over and inquire."

But Jennifer begged to follow in Danièlle's footsteps. She knew she could never be as beautiful as Danièlle but she wanted to try to be like her. During the past year she had come home from Toronto on a few occasions and the two girls always spent long hours together. Jennifer saved up her questions for Danièlle who patiently answered them all. She told her that at the school she could study her regular subjects as well as take two or three ballet classes a day. Jennifer had questioned her particularly about mime. "It's a way of talking with your body," Danièlle said. "You can tell a whole story without saying a word."

In a few days, after many more discussions with her family, Jennifer posted a letter written by her mother requesting an audition at the school. "I guess there's no harm in writing a letter," her mother had said, "but you would be wise not to expect too much."

* * *

Three weeks had passed and still there was no reply from the school in Toronto. Each day Jennifer would race home from school at noon, just in time to see the mailman, Mr. Blais, coming down the path and whistling cheerfully. "Nothing from Toronto today," he'd say as though it were a big joke. After a while Jennifer stopped coming home for lunch. She had almost given up hope of ever hearing from the school but she tried to hide her disappointment from her family.

"Mother warned you not to expect too much," her sister Sue reminded her.

"I know," Jennifer shrugged. "I'm not expecting anything."

At the end of the fifth week Jennifer came home from school later than usual. She and Anna sauntered into the house.

"Mum, could we have some cookies?"

"No need to shout," her mother called. "I'm right here." She appeared with a letter in her hand. "Are you sure you wouldn't like to read this first?"

"Is it from Toronto?" Anna burst out in excitement. "Read it aloud! What does it say?"

This was a moment that Jennifer would have liked to have all to herself but she took the crisp white sheet in her shaking hands and began to read:

Dear Mrs. Allen,
Audition class for girls and boys of ages ten to twelve will be held Saturday, May 1st, at two o'clock. All girls are requested to wear short-sleeved black leotards, white socks and pink ballet slippers. Their hair must be neatly tied back with no bows or ornaments. Absolutely no jewellery, including watches, will be allowed.

Please bring all school reports for the current year with you.

Yours truly,

Mary Collins,
Assistant Principal.

Chapter Five

*J*ennifer could not believe it when she and her mother arrived at the school in Toronto on the first day of May. There was a long line-up outside for the audition. It stretched down the street and around the corner, just like at a movie.

"Don't worry," Mrs. Allen reassured her as they took their place at the end, "we have our letter."

Jennifer looked in awe at the school building. It resembled a castle. She heard a man in front of them tell his children that it dated back over a hundred years. "It's one of the oldest mansions in Toronto," he explained. "And to save it from being torn down the city eventually donated it to the Professional School of Ballet."

The grey stone building stirred Jennifer's imagination. "I wonder who lived here all those years ago?" she

whispered to her mother. How she longed to explore every room!

There must have been one hundred and fifty boys and girls waiting outside. Jennifer counted seventy-eight in front and then gave up when she turned to see how many people had gathered behind. Some of the children looked as excited as she was, but others seemed afraid or even resentful. Jennifer noticed one girl pulling away from her mother who kept coaxing her. Further down the line another child was crying. Jennifer couldn't help staring at the shy and gloomy faces, then at these children's parents who had the eager eyes.

At last the oak doors were opened and everyone filed in one by one. Each child was given a number with the name and the age written beneath. Jennifer's number was seventy-nine. Somehow it sounded lucky, especially when she repeated it to herself over and over again. All the children were told to go downstairs and get changed while their parents were interviewed. Jennifer looked over at her mother who gave her an encouraging smile, then she followed the other girls into the dressing room.

Everything Jennifer needed was ready in her red plaid bag. Her black leotard still fit her, and she wriggled into it, smoothing out every crease. Her ballet slippers were brand-new because she had outgrown the ones from London. She fitted them on over her clean white socks, securing them with the white elastic so the shoes would not slip off her feet. Jennifer's hair was already pinned up in a neat little chignon. Her mother had done it for her early that morning before they had left Sault Ste. Marie.

"Oh, can't I just put a bow around?" Jennifer had pleaded, holding a long silk ribbon, but her mother had reminded her of the letter forbidding any ornaments. Remembering those instructions, Jennifer now removed her watch and the good-luck charm she had around her neck.

First she had to go for an interview with the headmistress of the school section. Her mother sat beside her as Jennifer handed her report cards to a friendly lady called Miss Blake, whose flaming red hair bounced around in tight little curls. She kept looking up and smiling at Jennifer as she read the reports, then she asked a few questions.

"Well, I'm satisfied. You're obviously a very bright girl," she said. "But of course you'll also have to please the ballet department."

Jennifer experienced her first real pang of nervousness and Miss Blake smiled kindly at her worried face.

"Just do the very best you can," she said.

Next they were sent to the school nurse, Miss Harris. This woman was not at all like the headmistress, Miss Blake. She was stern and businesslike. She tested Jennifer's heart and blood pressure, and checked all her muscles and joints.

"Has she had the measles or mumps?" she asked Jennifer's mother, then she scribbled something on a form and dismissed them.

Jennifer was now led into a ballet studio and her mother was told that she would have to wait about an hour and a half. The boys had been sent to another studio; only the girls were being auditioned here. The huge room was mirrored on all sides, with barres attached. A young teacher directed Jennifer to a place at the barre. "We'll be starting in about ten minutes," she said.

Nervously Jennifer looked around. There were about fifty girls in the studio. Although they were all shapes and sizes, she guessed they must have been about her age. In the corners of the room she spotted the resin boxes, then she noticed the piano, and it made her think of Mr. Vincent. Jennifer fought to dispel that ugly memory. In the front of the room she counted ten chairs; as she watched, important-looking people kept coming in, taking their seats and preparing their pads and pencils. A very small lady dressed in pink chiffon then made her entrance and took the centre position.

"That's Madame Rose. She's the principal of the school," Jennifer heard a girl whisper.

As Madame Rose sat down she scrutinized the children, speaking softly to the woman beside her.

The room was called to order with a sharp clap of someone's hands. Uneasy stillness replaced the nervous buzzing. The children stood awkwardly in fidgety silence while the ten examiners looked them over, commenting among themselves. Why were they taking so long in looking? Jennifer wondered, and she watched their faces anxiously. Suddenly she sensed that she was being appraised and she didn't know what to do. She tried to appear casual while staring at her toes but she could feel her face burning with embarrassment. After a while a younger teacher quietly approached some of the girls, asking that they step aside and just watch the class.

Jennifer noticed that these girls were all rather plump, and she remembered what Danièlle had once told her about dancers having to be thin.

The remaining students were directed to stand in rows while each was examined by one of the ten teachers. A man with friendly blue eyes came up to Jennifer.

"Please stretch your feet," he said, then he took her ankles and rotated them. Next he twisted her knees, bending her legs in funny directions. He kept making little jokes and Jennifer, who was so nervous, had to bite her tongue to stop from giggling hysterically.

"Now let's see if your muscles are flexible enough," he said. Jennifer was instructed to hold onto the barre and stand on one leg while he lifted the other one to see how high it would go – to the front, to the side and to the back. "Very good," he said when he lifted her leg to the back. "You're going to have a nice arabesque." But she knew she was stiff when he raised her leg to the front. Something hurt along the back of her leg when he tried to force it higher.

Next the teacher tested her back. Standing behind her, he took hold of her shoulders and bent her sideways from the waist, forward, then gently backward. As she was being pulled back, Jennifer's eyes filled with dizzying lights and she was thankful for the examiner's strong hand which supported her when she arched.

"You have a loose back," he said, "but you're going to have to work very hard to make it strong."

He asked her to raise her arms, then he wound them forward and backward from the shoulder sockets. Lastly, he took her head and rolled it gently forward from the neck then around in a circle. Jennifer relaxed, thinking he was finished, but back her head went and now he was turning it in the other direction. She felt like a puppet.

"Okay, thank you," he said. He gave her a wink and moved on to the next girl.

"Wow!" There were still a few spots in Jennifer's eyes making her dizzy. She had never before felt her body move in such funny directions. When the testing was over Jennifer noticed that many more girls were asked to stand at the side. Half an hour later there were only twenty girls left in the room. The assistant principal, Miss Collins, now started a class with music. The girls had to do very slow exercises sitting on the floor and standing at the barre. Jennifer followed as best she could, but from time to time one of the young teachers came over and helped her find the right position. The rest of the examiners sat on their chairs up front, whispering, watching and pointing, and busily writing on their pads.

To Jennifer's relief it was not hard to understand Miss Collins as she taught the exercises. Very clearly she explained the five positions of the feet and as she demonstrated each move, Jennifer watched intently. But occasionally she couldn't resist glancing over at Madame Rose. She knew that this awesome lady had been a famous ballerina many years ago. Her white hair was still piled high into a dancer's bun on the top of her head. There were many lines in her face yet her piercing eyes did not seem old. She fixed them on each girl in the class, never shifting her gaze as she whispered comments to the other examiners.

She looks very strict, thought Jennifer. I wonder what she's saying about me.

In a little while Miss Collins went over to join in the discussions. The studio doors were opened and the students started filing out of the room. As Jennifer lingered, she heard Miss Collins quietly asking a few girls to stay behind. Dismayed, she rushed for the stairs, when – "Number seventy-nine! Number seventy-nine!" a voice called in the doorway. Turning, she saw the nice man who had examined her.

"Jennifer, what's your hurry?" he said.

Back she came into the studio with great joy in her heart. Well, she wasn't out yet! Jennifer and five others were now tested for their musicality. They were given clapping rhythms which, one at a time, they had to copy and stamp back with their feet. Jennifer stumbled a little but she thought she got a few of them right.

At last the audition was over and the girls were told to go downstairs and change back into their clothes. Anxiously Jennifer searched the faces of Miss Collins and Madame Rose for a sign as to how she had done, but they were talking very seriously and once Jennifer thought Madame Rose had given her an angry look.

It was very quiet in the dressing room with just six girls after the number that had changed there at the beginning of the day. Jennifer's mother was waiting for her as she came back up the stairs.

"Well, Jenny, how did you do?" she asked eagerly. But Jennifer hardly dared look at her mother. She couldn't say anything because she really didn't know.

Part II

Chapter Six

*A*s Jennifer awoke, her eyes focussed on an unfamiliar crack in the ceiling. Blinking away the sleep, she slowly became aware of rhythmic breathing from the beds beside her. Now she remembered where she was! Hadn't she looked forward to her first day of school for the last three months? Jennifer would never forget the triumph in her mother's voice the day the letter of acceptance arrived from Toronto.

"Oh, Jenny, you did it! You're in!" she cried.

Jennifer's bags were ready long in advance of yesterday's journey, for it was to be the first time she had ever travelled alone. Unfortunately she had been the very last one to arrive at the Student House in Toronto. It was after midnight and the mistress in charge had created quite a fuss about it. But Jennifer was too exhausted to even explain that the train from Sault Ste. Marie had broken down and there had been no one to meet her at the station. Luckily Jennifer had her destination written down "just in case," and she found a taxi with a very nice driver.

"I love the ballet," he said when she gave him the address of the school's Student House. "I go whenever I can, although it's difficult because I work nights. My favourite ballet is *Swan Lake*. What's yours?"

"*Cinderella*," Jennifer replied. She didn't say that it was the only ballet she had ever seen.

"Oh, yeah, that's a nice one too. What's your name?"

Jennifer hesitated. Her mother had warned her not to talk to strangers in the big city, but this man liked ballet so surely that was different. "Jennifer Allen," she replied.

"Well, Jennifer Allen, I'll remember your name and maybe one day I'll see you on stage."

Jennifer nodded her head in doubt and hope. She didn't quite know what to say except "Thank you," then the driver pulled up at the door of a large house.

"This is it," he announced cheerfully. "Your new home."

Jennifer peered nervously out of the car window. It was too dark to see much but she noticed that the building was very old. The driver carried her suitcases to the door and she almost wished he wouldn't leave. He rang the bell, then patted her on the head. "Good luck, Jennifer," he said. He'd already driven off when Jennifer realized she hadn't paid him any cab fare.

"Oh, dear!" she said out loud. "I wonder if I'll ever see

him again?" Then summoning up her courage, she pressed the buzzer again.

* * *

With a huge yawn, Jennifer sat up in bed to investigate her new surroundings in the morning light. She recalled having trudged up an endless number of stairs to the fifth floor, and she could see now that her room was in the attic. It was shaped more like a passageway. Two walls sloped steeply to a point; at one end they framed the pine door and at the other, a lattice window. Through its diamond-shaped panes the sun shot patterns all over the room. Almost all the space was occupied by three beds lined up in a row. Jennifer had been left the one in the middle although she would have much preferred to be near the window.

She turned over to examine the freckled face of her sleeping neighbour, Emily Stock. Even though it was after midnight when she arrived, the girls had exchanged whispered information in the dark room. Emily was from Edmonton and she was two months, three weeks and nine days older than Jennifer. She had studied dancing for two and a half years and was the star of her ballet school back home. In the bed on Jennifer's left, huddled under twisted sheets and blankets, lay a girl named Suzanne. She had flown here yesterday all the way from Vancouver. Jennifer didn't know much about her because Suzanne wouldn't even answer when Emily asked her how long she had studied ballet; but later Jennifer heard her stifled sobs from under the pillow and she understood.

Suddenly there was a loud rapping at the door. It

woke up Emily and Suzanne who opened their eyes with the same bewilderment as Jennifer had a short while ago.

"It's time, girls. Come on, it's time," a woman's voice shrilled. "Hurry, hurry, only five minutes to breakfast!" The woman who burst into the room was the one who had reprimanded Jennifer for being late last night. "Well, girls, morning, morning. I'm Mrs. Peers," she announced importantly. "It's time you were up, you know. High time. Now there'll be no nonsense from you small ones. *No nonsense*. Just do what I tell you, obey the rules, and there won't be trouble."

Jennifer jumped up, watching out of the corner of her eye as Mrs. Peers loomed over Suzanne's bed. The lady in starchy white was not tall but she had large hands and a jutting jaw. Pink scalp showed through her pin curls and her creased face was heavily powdered.

"You're my youngest charges," she said as the girls hurriedly began to dress. "I mean business! So remember, there'll be no nonsense from you." She glared at Jennifer, who quickly avoided her narrowed eyes by darting to her heaving chest. It hadn't even occurred to Jennifer until now that she might misbehave.

When the girls arrived in the dining room downstairs they saw a long pine table all laid for breakfast. The students were seated in order of seniority. Even though Suzanne was the youngest, Jennifer was the smallest and was placed at the end of the table. About ten new girls and boys, looking as shy and frightened as Jennifer felt, swallowed their toast. Compared to the breakfast of pancakes with maple syrup that she had gobbled up in Sault

Ste. Marie only yesterday, this meal was quite sparing. Each student was given one piece of toast, one poached egg and a glass of milk. Emily, who was sitting next to Jennifer, munched on her toast and remarked, "It looks like they're very weight conscious here. Before I was accepted I had to lose five pounds."

"Oh, how awful!" sympathized Jennifer, relieved that she had escaped such an order. "Then won't we even have desserts?" she asked worriedly. She was thinking of the candies and cakes and cookies she loved.

"Oh, no," said a boy named Peter, a second-year student sitting nearby. "We just have fruit here every night. It gets very boring. You should do what I do. Ask your parents to send you cookies."

Suddenly Jennifer spotted Danièlle who was sitting at the far end of the table with the senior students. She was waving to Jennifer and gave her a big wink. Jennifer beamed back and hoped the other students had noticed.

After breakfast Jennifer walked beside Emily and they joined a long line of children winding round the corner to the main school building. When she caught sight of the mansion, Jennifer was once again impressed by it. She climbed the wide stone steps clutching her red plaid bag and realized with pride that she now belonged here, that she, Jennifer Allen, was a student at the Professional School of Ballet in Toronto.

The vestibule was teeming with students; some in ecstatic reunion, others silently studying the schedules pinned up on the notice board. Amidst the confusion,

Jennifer was handed her own timetable by a lady with curly red hair.

"Hello, Jennifer," she said warmly, "welcome to the school."

At once Jennifer recognized the headmistress who had been the first to interview her and who didn't even seem to mind her arithmetic marks.

"Hi, Miss Blake," Jennifer replied, relieved to find a familiar face.

The students were funnelling through a narrow door into the large ballet studio where Jennifer had auditioned four months ago. They were directed to sit on the floor and Jennifer took her place with the grade five students in the front row, right under the noses of the staff who were seated facing them. There were a great number of teachers; Jennifer counted three rows of ten. She picked out Miss Collins, the assistant principal, and Mr. Young, the nice man who had examined her at the audition and had made her giggle. Then Jennifer watched Madame Rose, the principal. She was sitting in the centre, writing on her pad and eyeing the children exactly as she had done at the audition. Suddenly their eyes met and Jennifer, unsure of how to react, flushed deep red. But the look only lasted for a second, then the piercing black eyes fastened onto Emily beside her, and then moved on to the next student. It was as though Madame Rose wanted to penetrate into the mind of each child. What is she looking for? Jennifer asked herself uncomfortably.

A hush came over the studio as soon as Madame Rose stood up.

"Now that we are all assembled, I would like to welcome you to the school." Her voice was surprisingly soft. "You are all here because you want to dance. It is possible that some of you may become professional dancers. Others will discover that they prefer to do other things. I can only say that whatever you decide to do, each of you must work as hard as you can in order to succeed." Madame Rose paused. "You will hear the word 'discipline' a great deal here. I want every student in this room to understand the meaning of this word."

Jennifer, who was watching intently, felt as though the principal were talking directly to her. She wanted to dance, she knew that, and she would study hard, but she wasn't quite sure what Madame Rose meant. She glanced over at Emily but found no reaction, then she swallowed her doubts and looked around the ballet studio for comfort. On one wall there was a board displaying newspaper clippings of former students who had become famous. Maybe one day –

After Madame Rose had finished her speech she introduced each one of the teachers. At ten o'clock the students were dismissed and told to consult their timetables for their first lesson of the day.

"Don't be late," warned Madame Rose. "Punctuality is extremely important here. We have a lot to accomplish at this school in too little time."

Jennifer studied the sheet that Miss Blake had given her. It looked like a complicated puzzle, the kind she could never figure out. Emily managed to decipher it, pinpointing Monday; that was today. There was not a ballet class until eleven-forty-five. Before that there was a history lesson, which would start in five minutes.

"Let's go right up to the classroom and get desks next to each other," suggested Emily. "I know where the grade five room is – it's on the second floor."

Chapter Seven

*A*ccording to the timetable, Mr. Young taught the beginner's class on Mondays, but when Jennifer and Emily entered Studio Four at eleven-forty that first day, they found Miss Collins waiting for them. The ballet class had been divided into two groups, boys and girls, and the boys were lucky enough to have Mr. Young this morning. Jennifer was a little afraid of Miss Collins. She wasn't sure why, but she remembered feeling that way at the audition. Perhaps it was because this very tall woman with the short blond hair looked so determined, as if she had an arduous task to perform in teaching ballet to beginners.

Miss Collins commenced by demonstrating all the basic exercises which were necessary in order to learn how to dance. Facing the barre the girls learned various exercises for their knees and feet which they had to repeat over and over again. At the same time Miss Collins taught them the names which were all in French. Looking over the girls, she chose Jennifer as a model to help her demonstrate the theory of "turn-out."

"This is one of the most important features of a ballet dancer's technique," she said. "Imagine that there is a brick wall right in front of your hips so that your feet, knees and thighs are forced to face sideways. The important thing to remember is that turn-out begins at the top of your legs. When you bend your knees, they must point in an imaginary line to your little toe."

With the help of Miss Collins, Jennifer managed to manoeuvre her knees sideways into the correct position, but they didn't want to stay there on their own. Miss Collins gave Jennifer's stomach a sharp tap. "Keep your tummy flat and firm and it will be a lot easier for you," she said. "There are many helpful muscles in your stomach that you must develop. They should be kept strong at all times – even when you're not dancing . . ." Miss Collins addressed the rest of the class.

Jennifer's eyes widened; she'd been holding her breath and was about to explode.

"Even when you're waiting for a bus," Miss Collins continued. She caught sight of Jennifer's purple face. "Oh, my!" she burst out laughing. "You can breathe, dear." Jennifer let go with relief but unfortunately her tummy released also. "Aha! But you must learn to use all your muscles independently," insisted Miss Collins. She looked at Jennifer. "Pull in, but please don't ever stop breathing, for any reason."

Best of all Miss Collins liked the use of the arms in dancing, and for the next half hour the class stood in front of the mirror studying the line and form of their arms and their five basic positions.

"I want those arms to tell stories," Miss Collins said. "They must describe all kinds of beautiful images when you dance. And I won't tolerate flapping wrists or over-stretched elbows. Your arms must move with flowing softness."

Miss Collins then moved her arms in time with the music, while the students copied her movements. At one point Emily rolled her eyes in boredom at Jennifer; she had studied all of this already. But Jennifer was rather enjoying it. She could imagine things and make pictures with her arms.

"Make waves, like the lapping of water," Miss Collins had said, and Jennifer had only to think of the rolling sea to understand what Miss Collins meant.

"That's coming, Jennifer," her teacher singled her out again. "Now let's see you do the same thing standing in first position with those feet turned out and that tummy pulled in."

This presented some difficulties, for the minute Jennifer attempted to exercise control over her legs and body, her arms went rigid like two stiff boards.

Miss Collins consulted the round clock. "For the last ten minutes we shall do some stretches," she announced, and Jennifer was surprised to see it was already one o'clock. Oh, dear, she thought to herself, and we still haven't done any real dancing. Jennifer wasn't sure what Miss Collins meant by "stretches," but they didn't sound as if they would be much fun.

"Let's sit down," Miss Collins suggested in a commanding voice, and the girls slowly dropped to the floor, wondering what was coming next. This time Miss Collins chose a girl named Maureen to demonstrate, and Jennifer couldn't resist a twinge of disappointment. She had rather hoped that Miss Collins had taken a special liking to her.

"Clasp your feet," Miss Collins said, and she pushed Maureen's back forward, bouncing her head onto her knees. "Good!" she exclaimed. "Please look, girls. Maureen does this extremely well."

Jennifer attempted to do the same, but how it hurt! She couldn't straighten her legs like Maureen and her head wouldn't bounce anywhere near her knees. Her struggles did not escape Miss Collins' eyes and the teacher came over to help. "Ouch!" blurted Jennifer as quietly as she could, but Miss Collins would not stop pushing.

"You've got to learn to loosen up all those tight muscles," she said firmly, and Jennifer gritted her teeth as her head bobbed nearer and nearer her aching knees.

Next came the splits. Jennifer was dismayed to see the smug-looking Maureen perform these with no trouble at all; but the muffled grunts and groans, concealed in coughs, which came from the other students were of some comfort to Jennifer.

"All right. I want you to practise these exercises without fail every day." Brushing her black skirt, Miss Collins finally stood up. "They will become less difficult in

time," she added less sternly as she looked at the exhausted faces of her beginners' class. "Thank you. That's all for today."

Jennifer's first ballet lesson was over, and now she had an idea of the amount of work that lay ahead. She had learned a lot today but, most of all, she had found how little she could do. Dawdling, she picked up her bag. She was reluctant to hurry out of the room after her classmates because the next class was just beginning and she wanted to watch these older students. As she left the room she noticed that they were starting their class with one of the exercises she had learned. The dancers had one hand placed on the barre and they were bending their knees in an exercise that Miss Collins had called *pliés*.

That evening Danièlle told Jennifer that ballet dancers all over the world begin their day's training in exactly the same way. "It doesn't matter whether you're a beginner or a professional. Every ballet class you take for the rest of your life will start with *pliés*," Danièlle said. "Don't worry, Jennifer, you really are learning how to dance."

* * *

Every day from nine in the morning until six at night Jennifer was absorbed in her school work. There were times when laziness crept over her, but then she would remember the words of Madame Rose: "You are all here because you want to dance. Each of you must work as hard as you can and understand the meaning of the word discipline." Just thinking about this tiny woman who had been such a great dancer filled Jennifer with fresh determination. It did not take her long to realize that it was important to gain the ballet teacher's attention; being noticed was a sign of whether you had any talent. Some students were definitely singled out more than others, and as long as Jennifer kept working hard she was one of them.

With Maureen Anderson it was completely different. She was very pretty, but it was her long legs and arched feet that seemed to so impress the ballet staff. There were days when Miss Collins appeared uninterested in anyone else. Jennifer tried not to notice that Miss Collins merely corrected her while she often praised Maureen. For her part, Maureen did not seem very enthused about ballet. She pooh-poohed Miss Collins' seriousness and she did devastating imitations of Madame Rose in the dressing room. Yet in class she was always the first to master new steps. Her body naturally flowed into the right positions and Miss Collins chose her most often to demonstrate to the rest of the class. It just didn't seem fair to Jennifer that she, who really cared, had to work so much harder.

Jennifer's model at the school was Danièlle, and many times she was shooed away from cracks in the door when she peeked at her dancing with the graduate students. She knew that Danièlle was considered one of the most talented dancers in the school and that next year she might be accepted in the performing company. No matter how involved Danièlle was, she always found time to comfort her little friend from Sault Ste. Marie. "Don't feel discouraged, Jenny. It takes time to become a dancer. Don't forget, you're training your body to do unnatural things in the most beautiful way possible, and that can't be done overnight. It's taken me nine years, and here you are, impatient after two weeks!"

Danièlle often cheered Jennifer up by telling her news about their neighbours in Sault Ste. Marie. "My mother isn't called the neighbourhood gossip for nothing," she'd say, waving a letter. "Just listen to this!" And she always succeeded in making Jennifer smile, even when her stories rambled and Jennifer suspected she wasn't reading at all. She was sure that Danièlle had made up the story about Mr. Vincent's new toupee, but she giggled all the same.

Jennifer still felt the need to slip away to a private place to sort out her problems or to try to share her new world in a letter to her family, but almost without fail Mrs. Peers would find her. "Aha!" she would sputter in triumph. "I've caught you sneaking off again! What are you up to?" She refused to listen to Jennifer's explanations of wanting to be alone. "You're up to some mischief," she'd say, her finger wagging and her chest heaving. "I know it and I'm going to put a stop to it."

Jennifer grew more and more upset as the days went by. She became convinced that Mrs. Peers had singled her out and was spying on her wherever she went. Other girls seemed to get away with little tricks but she was always caught.

One day after lunch she was on her way downstairs when Jennifer heard voices in the living room. Mrs. Peers' voice rang out strongly. "There's something strange about that girl. I mean, why is she always hiding? It's just not natural." Jennifer froze. She knew that Mrs. Peers was talking about her. Who else was in the room? she wondered. She felt embarrassed, then angry. She did not want to be ridiculed in front of her other teachers.

"Oh, no, no . . . " There were muttered protests. "Why, Jennifer is the hardest worker in my class," said someone. "I'd say she was an excellent student." It was Miss Collins. Jennifer gripped the banister. Those words would have made her so happy any other time.

"Yes, you know she doesn't have much of a head for figures, yet I do believe she tries as hard as she can." That was Mrs. Owen, Jennifer's mathematics teacher, and her remarks were met with murmurs of approval. "Hard to believe we're talking about the same person," Mrs. Peers said, and at that moment she appeared in the doorway. "You little monster!" she shrieked on seeing Jennifer. "Look at that! What did I tell you?" she shouted into the living room, shaking her steel clips. "She was *eavesdropping*!"

Jennifer fled, trying not to think of what her other teachers would be saying about her now.

Chapter Eight

One Tuesday morning a few weeks later, Jennifer was running as fast as she could down the street towards the school. The time was five minutes to nine and she was terrified that she might be late for class.

Once a week the beginners started the day with their ballet lesson, taught by Miss Collins who always seemed particularly solemn at that hour of the morning.

Jennifer raced up the stone steps and into the school building. She had only two minutes. The trouble was that she still had to get changed. One thing she had already discovered about a dancing life was the number of times in one day she was required to change her clothes. It seemed to never end! Today she would be getting dressed, undressed, and dressed again eight times! Danièlle had chuckled when Jennifer complained to her about it. "C'est la vie," she had said,

68

"that's life. Let's hope one day it will be costumes you'll be putting on."

One minute to go as Jennifer tore into the dressing room. She ripped open her red plaid bag which was beginning to look really torn, and she almost jumped into her practise clothes. Hastily she patted her bun which was nailed down with pins, and started towards the classroom. *Oops!* Her shoes. Jennifer ran back and wriggled her feet into her pink leather ballet slippers, then made her way as fast as she could to the studio. The big clock at the top of the stairs pointed to one minute past nine.

Miss Collins didn't even notice Jennifer tiptoeing in. She was much too involved in conversation with some very special visitors to the class. Jennifer spotted them immediately, her eyes widening in amazement. It was obvious from the looks on everyone's faces that the two boys and two girls talking to Miss Collins were very important people. They were certainly not just senior students. Could they possibly be professional dancers from the Performing Company? It was almost too awesome for Jennifer to imagine. But why would they ever want to take such a simple class as hers?

Edging over behind Emily, the girls exchanged quick, silent looks which confirmed Jennifer's guess. She was filled with nervous excitement. How was she ever going to be able to learn the exercises, or to even listen to what Miss Collins was saying?

Jennifer scrutinized the visitors. You could tell they weren't students just by what they wore. The taller girl had her blond hair tied in a crimson scarf and she wore a matching leotard. The other girl had on a bright-yellow leotard with black tights, and Jennifer was surprised to see that her hair was cut very short. She had just assumed that all dancers were required to have long hair. The boys wore striped T-shirts and they had a funny assortment of knitted woollens on their legs. One of them even wore a pair of the blue-and-white Maple Leaf hockey socks, but he must have had a sore muscle, for he wore both of them on the same leg. Jennifer gazed enviously at their cheerful colours. School students were only allowed to wear black leotards and pink tights; and the "little ones" like Jennifer were required to wear white socks, much to her mortification.

While Miss Collins fussed about finding her guests a place at the barre, Jennifer edged closer to Emily. "Why would they take a beginner's class?" she whispered.

"They've just returned from a long tour," Emily told her, "and they're very tired. I heard them tell Miss Collins they wanted a class that was basic and simple."

"Oh." Jennifer was puzzled. She, who was eager to dispense with exercises so that she could really start dancing, found it strange that these professionals should choose to do the opposite.

A sharp clap of Miss Collins' hands brought order to the room. She looked less severe today as she surveyed her larger class.

"Would you step back, Jennifer, and let Miss Brook stand in front of you," she ordered.

Jennifer readily made room for the blond girl who smiled with a hint of apology as she placed herself at the barre in front of Jennifer. Miss Collins then demonstrated a series of the traditional pliés in first, second and fifth positions, and the lesson began.

Jennifer could not believe her luck. It was just like the kind of dream story she usually made up. Here was a real-live professional dancer doing the same exercises to the same music right in front of her! Jennifer chuckled inwardly. No, even she couldn't have imagined anything quite as exciting as this. She glued her eyes to the girl in front. She wanted to copy her exactly, and she concentrated with every muscle in her body. For the first time ever, Jennifer managed a plié in fifth position without a wobble. This was quite an achievement. Inspired, she took her hand off the barre just as Miss Brook was doing, but unlike her model, Jennifer teetered dangerously, swaying backwards and then forwards, her arms waving until she clutched at the supporting rail again.

It looks so easy, she thought ruefully, and trying to regain her balance she pulled in her stomach muscles so tightly that they felt as if they must be touching all the way back to her spine.

Any exercise done on the right side had to be repeated on the left, so that both legs would be trained equally. When she had to turn around, Jennifer pretended that Miss Brook was still in front of her and that she, Jennifer, was her shadow.

As the class continued, Jennifer became more impressed by the seriousness with which this professional dancer worked. She seemed to have an inner purpose that had nothing to do with trying to please the teacher. Every time she checked herself sideways in the mirror to ensure that her head, shoulders, ribs and hips were in a straight line, Jennifer did the same. Whenever Miss Brook repeated the foot exercises and held a position long after the music had stopped, Jennifer tried this too, although it was hard to ignore the cramps this extra work produced in the arches of her feet.

Guiltily Jennifer thought of how she sometimes resorted to holding an incorrect position on purpose so that she would be noticed by Miss Collins. She was often obsessed with a need for attention; that was how she could be reassured that her teacher cared. Now Jennifer realized that she had only been cheating herself and she vowed never to do that again. Miss Brook, in fact, listened attentively to every comment the teacher made, even if another dancer was being corrected.

For the first time since coming to the school, Jennifer began to comprehend why she was being forced to learn correct ballet technique. Here was a dancer who could do all the difficult things Miss Collins demanded. Up until now Jennifer hadn't been entirely convinced that such details were really possible. But Miss Brook's hips were turned out, her feet were pointed, her knees were straight and, wonder of wonders, her stomach was flat. Her barre work was polished and controlled. It was beautiful to watch. It suddenly dawned on Jennifer that Miss Brook was dancing even though she appeared to be doing only exercises at a barre. It was obvious that she and other professional dancers would never be finished perfecting their training exercises no matter how often they performed on stage.

I guess this is what Danièlle has been trying to tell

me, Jennifer mused. She now understood that there could be no fine dancing without basic technique. But, she wondered, will I ever be patient enough?

"Jennifer!" Miss Collins called out in alarm. "Why is your chin jutting forward like that? And your shoulders are up around your ears!"

A quick glance in the mirror confirmed Miss Collins' words, and Jennifer stood helplessly as her teacher rushed over to poke and prod her into the correct stance. If only her body would do what her mind told it! She sighed. But then again, Danièlle would say, "It's going to take a few more years."

Miss Brook had made a lasting impression on Jennifer. She now knew how she would like to dance and the way to go about it. Nothing but hard work would give her that ease and grace.

"I can do it!" Deep within herself, Jennifer knew she could. She felt inspired by the irresistible challenge. Her spirits soared as today the class sped by.

Looking up at the clock, Miss Collins said, "You've done well, children." It was the first time she'd ever said that. "And I'm sure we shall all remember the lessons we've learned from our distinguised visitors." Jennifer nodded her head vigorously.

As the class disbanded, the four dancers picked up their big leather bags and went over to shake hands with Miss Collins. Jennifer couldn't take her eyes off them. No, she thought, I won't forget their visit. I shall pretend that Miss Brook is standing in front of me in every class from now on.

"Come on," Emily was tugging at her arm, "we'll be

late for math. if you don't hurry. Miss Collins went overtime again."

Jennifer followed her friend downstairs to the dressing room. There was never any time to lose. She could already tell that this was going to be one of those days when she was late for everything. She knew from experience that once she got behind she could never catch up.

Chapter Nine

*J*ennifer's days as a student and a dancer were crammed with lessons, and each hour was regulated by the complicated timetable that she always carried with her. There was no time for dawdling, no time to do anything but dash from one class to the next. Jennifer often found herself thinking of her little hideaway in the garden in Sault Ste. Marie, and she worried that her father might clean it up while she was away. What a comfort it had been to escape there – to do nothing, to dream of everything without having to explain yourself.

As the weeks passed, Jennifer dragged herself out of bed later each morning. She had long ago blocked out Mrs. Peers' insistent morning calls. Many times she missed breakfast altogether, but she could always count on Emily to save her a muffin.

The dark circles under her eyes should have given

away her secret. With money saved, Jennifer had bought a flashlight and this made it possible for her to stay up far into the night. Those were her favourite times, when in the stillness the whole house slept while she felt like the only person in the world. She was free to read, to write or to dream. Sometimes she even dared to venture downstairs for something to eat, but only when she was certain she heard snores from behind Mrs. Peers' door.

Mornings came too soon and today, as usual, Jennifer had overslept. She blinked at her big red clock which clearly said quarter to nine, and she leapt out of bed. With lightning speed she dressed and brushed her teeth, but it was fixing her hair for ballet class that slowed Jennifer down. She fumbled and fussed, furious with herself for her clumsiness. She could hear Emily calling to her from downstairs, which made her even more exasperated. For each pin that went in, another slipped out. How many times had Mrs. Peers and Emily shown Jennifer how to make a ponytail and then twist it into a small, neat knot? But whenever Jennifer tried it by herself she would end up with an oversized bun encrusted with several packages of pins. Emily often teased her about her studded helmet, and the truth was that Jennifer's head weighed a ton. This had caused a problem with her pirouettes.

Only yesterday, Jennifer had had a ghastly experience. Madame Rose had come to watch ballet class. It was a rare occasion when the principal attended, and all the students worked hard to impress her. Jennifer had been having a good day and Mr. Young was very pleased with her work. "Jennifer," he had said, "I'd like you to demonstrate to the class your turns from the corner."

Jennifer's heart had sunk. This time she actually wished he had asked Maureen. At the best of times pirouettes were difficult, and although no one else may have noticed, the large lump on the back of her head had begun to wobble precariously. Nervously she stood in fifth position, her hands on her shoulders, knowing the eyes of the whole room were upon her and feeling those deep black eyes of Madame Rose. The music started and off Jennifer went, twirling then reeling across the studio. *Ping! Ping! Ping!* One by one the huge pins started to fly, scattering all over the room. For a moment even Madame Rose had to duck one of the zinging missiles headed in her direction.

Jennifer was mortified. Within seconds her hair was completely loose and the floor was covered with a mass of steel. Smirks were on everyone's lips and even Mr. Young could scarcely conceal a smile. Only Madame Rose did not look amused. For an unendurable length of time the class was disrupted gathering up the pins, then there was an awkward pause as Jennifer shuffled over to the mirror, attempting to repair the frizzy mess. Even though she hadn't the gumption to look into her own shamed eyes, she knew that her face was deep red.

"Hurry up, Jennifer!" yelled a voice from downstairs. Jennifer shivered. Her face burned just thinking of that awful incident.

"One more pin," she said, jabbing in two. Then she grabbed her coat and scarf and ran down the hall. She would see if she could find Danièlle before her ballet class today which wasn't till eleven-thirty. Danièlle was the only one left who could help her now.

Choosing the fastest route, Jennifer slid down the banister to the main floor. Emily was standing there beaming, instead of looking mad as Jennifer had expected. She waved a letter at her friend. "My mother's coming to visit for Thanksgiving weekend," she said excitedly. "She's never been to Toronto so we can show her around."

Jennifer felt a quick pang. It seemed like such a long time since she had seen her mother. She had now been at school for two months. "That's great, Emily," she said. "Maybe we could ask her if you can come to Sault Ste. Marie for Christmas."

Emily's face shone. "Oh, Jennifer, that would be fantastic, because I know she'll say yes!"

Funny to be thinking of Christmas already, mused Jennifer as the two girls raced off to school. But how wonderful it was going to be to see her family again. She ran with eagerness at such an encouraging thought. When she arrived at school Jennifer figured out the time on the calendar. Christmas vacation was still ten weeks away!

After a French lesson and a science test, for which Jennifer had not studied enough, it was time to get changed for ballet class. To Jennifer's relief she spotted Danièlle in the seniors' section of the dressing room. There was no need to explain her problem. Danièlle had already heard about it. It seemed yesterday's episode had been whispered all around the school.

"Look, Jennifer," said Danièlle, "your hair is like mine, very long and thick – "

"And frizzy," Jennifer interrupted bitterly.

"Well," said Danièlle, "you just have to train your hair the way you do the rest of your body. Here, try these special clips. They're stronger and better than bobby pins." Deftly Danièlle showed Jennifer a way of fastening her hair into a small knot at the nape of her neck with three strong clips. Her head suddenly felt free and no amount of shaking or tossing could loosen a single strand.

"Oh, Danièlle, thank you!" cried Jennifer, pirouetting with joy. "Thank you, thank you, thank you!"

Now Jennifer felt like a different person in her ballet class. Mr. Young was teaching again and he repeated most of the exercises from the day before. Jennifer liked that because then she could try and improve some of the mistakes she had made. She found that she was getting steadier and more in control of her body, although never as much as she would have liked. And lately she and Maureen seemed to be the two students in the class who received the most attention. Today her head felt light, released of its usual load, and even her turns from the corner were much improved.

"That's it, Jennifer," encouraged Mr. Young. "Keep your tummy in and your eyes glued to your spot."

"Spotting," Jennifer had learned, was very important. This was the secret that professional dancers knew to stop from getting dizzy when they executed spins and pirouettes. You had to choose a place on the wall and never take your eyes off it. The second you let your gaze wander, the room would reel around you. Staring at a smudge on the wall, Jennifer arrived safely at the corner, having completed a diagonal line. Behind her, Maureen spiralled in the same direction at a great speed. How did she do it? Maureen was just a natural turner, that was all. She never had any trouble with pirouettes.

Just then the door to the studio opened and in walked Madame Rose. This was the second day in a row that she had come to watch! Instinctively Jennifer's hand shot to the back of her head, but the wad of hair felt reassuringly secure. Jennifer hardly dared look at the lady as she passed by to sit up at the front of the room, but she could smell her perfume. To her astonishment she heard a quiet voice say to her, "How are you today, Jennifer?"

"F-f-fine, thank you," she stammered, quickly looking up, and there she saw a smile of such gentleness that the little girl blinked in amazement. Another second and it was gone. Madame Rose's face had returned to its customary sternness. Only her deep black eyes held the trace of warmth that Jennifer had just seen.

Mr. Young only had two more exercises to give the class before it was time to stop. One was the big jump they had done yesterday. Jennifer suddenly became nervous. She wanted to impress Madame Rose so much that she kept forgetting the exercise.

"Try it with a second group, Jennifer," Mr. Young said with an understanding look. "And this time use those feet to push yourself up into the air. Think of the ground as if it were covered with hot coals so that you'd burn the soles of your feet if you stayed there too long."

Jennifer pushed, jumped and bounced, all the time

imagining the burning coals. This time she got the steps right and she did them better. Still, that wasn't good enough and Jennifer ran around to the back to do the exercise again with the next group of dancers. Now and then she would check to see if Madame Rose was looking at her, but just like everyone else, she seemed to be watching Maureen.

To end the class, Mr. Young did leg kicks to the side, called *grand battements*. "Hips down, feet pointed," he sang out with the music. "Don't forget, you mustn't drop those legs. They must descend with the same control and at the same speed as they go up."

What he asked was extremely difficult, especially without the barre to hold onto. But ten unsteady pairs of legs tried their best, and the music had an accompaniment of shuffles and scrapes.

The lesson over, Mr. Young raised his hand before the group could disappear. "Madame Rose would like to speak to you," he announced.

The room hushed instantly. She stood up. "You are working well, class," she began, "and I'm pleased with your progress. As you may know, the Performing Company will be dancing at the Christmas season this year. They have asked the school to provide some of the extras for their performances here in Toronto. We'll be choosing two girls and three boys from this class," Madame Rose continued, "so keep on working and we shall make our decision in a couple of weeks. One more thing," she added. "By now you're well acquainted with the rules of the school. They must be obeyed. None of you will ever become dancers without discipline. I want you all to be much neater in appearance." She paused meaningfully. "Especially in ballet class. The girls may now wear pink tights instead of white socks, if they wish." There was a rustle of joy. "But," Madame Rose raised her voice, "no messy hair, no sloppy ribbons and no chewing gum."

Jennifer and Suzanne lowered their eyes and Emily stifled a gulp. The three girls knew whom their principal was addressing with these words.

Jennifer made fervent vows to transform herself into a model student. She would even try to reconcile with Mrs. Peers. To be chosen to perform with the company on stage was too much to hope for and she dared not even think about it. But deep inside, although she probably wouldn't have admitted it, she wished with all her heart that it might be her.

Chapter Ten

Thanksgiving weekend brought a bright Saturday afternoon. The cool air breezed through Jennifer's hair as she walked briskly down the street. She was on her way to the ballet shop with Emily and Mrs. Stock. Jennifer had liked her friend's mother at once. There was something about Mrs. Stock that made even the most ordinary things she said seem absurd, and the way she pronounced "bahlet" was so ridiculous that Jennifer had to choke back the giggles in order not to offend Emily. Still, it did feel good to chuckle again and throw off some of the weight of her serious ballet life.

As they hurried along, Jennifer couldn't stop thinking about the hilarious meeting between Madame Rose and Mrs. Stock. The women had eyed each other a trifle suspiciously and there had been an awkward pause. Jennifer, who had become an astute observer of Madame

Rose, sensed her dismay at Mrs. Stock's figure. There was no doubt about it, Emily's mother was a plump and portly lady. Breaking through the principal's reserve, Mrs. Stock had said in a voice far too loud, "Great to meet you, Miss Tulip. Emily's bent my ear about you." And everyone, even Madame Rose, had burst out laughing. Everyone, that is, except Emily, who had been mortified at her mother's blunder.

Seeing Mrs. Stock, Jennifer could now understand Emily's problem with her weight. Miss Collins had been merciless about her stomach and legs and Jennifer felt very sorry for her. She knew how difficult it was not to eat ravenously after a long, tiring day at school. In fact, Jennifer would sometimes sneak out in the late afternoon and buy half a dozen chocolate doughnuts at the bakery shop around the corner. As a friend she would have liked to share them with Emily but she knew it was far more considerate to eat them all herself.

The two girls had become very good friends. "It's because we're complete opposites," Emily would say. She was organized and reliable and if she hadn't been Jennifer's friend she would probably have been Mrs. Peers' pet. Everyone in the school liked Emily. She seemed to know how to handle both the teachers and the students, and there was many a time when she patched up a difficult situation for Jennifer. Night after night Jennifer would make firm resolutions to model herself after her friend, but by the light of day she could never manage to change herself for very long.

"Where is this place?" panted Mrs. Stock, her breath

coming out in great puffs. In their eagerness the two girls had been racing ahead.

"Oh, Mom, only about three more blocks," apologized Emily. "I'm sorry, I didn't realize it was so far. We'll take the subway home. I want you to see it, anyway."

Jennifer didn't mind the long walk even though her legs ached from her two ballet classes that morning. She felt very happy. At last she was going to have pink tights like those professional and senior dancers wore. Her mother had sent her enough money for two pairs. Jennifer secretly wondered if she could buy just one pair and get a new ballet bag with the rest of the money. She had saved her allowance for the last three weeks but she didn't know if it would be enough. Of course, she still liked her English red plaid bag, but the clasp was broken and the handle was gone and a large hole had appeared in the bottom.

"Here we are. Oooh, look!" breathed Emily, pressing her face right against the shop window.

One glance and Jennifer realized she would never have enough money for all the things she would want to buy. The window was displayed with tights and leotards in every imaginable colour, some even sparkled with sequins.

"O-o-o-h-h," gasped Mrs. Stock. "Fishnet stockings!" She was pressed right up to the glass beside the two girls. "I wore those years ago when I did my tap numbers," she said, dreamy with nostalgia.

Jennifer giggled and glanced at Emily who did not laugh. Then she spotted a row of pink satin pointe shoes. "Too bad we aren't coming to buy those, eh, Emily?"

"Oh, Jennifer, you're never satisfied. Come on, let's go in." Emily marched quickly into the shop, with Jennifer and Mrs. Stock hurrying close behind.

It was like stepping into another world. Smith's Theatrical Supplies was a very busy place on a Saturday afternoon. The shop was filled with parents and children, all intoxicated with the glamour of their surroundings. Jennifer had always loved to dress up in her mother's cast-off clothes, but here was a store where they sold glittering costumes made for that purpose. Here was the world of make-believe! Jennifer's dazzled eyes took in wigs, moustaches, masks, noses, top hats and batons. There were outfits for clowns, policemen, dwarfs and duchesses.

Jennifer wandered over to the make-up counter, where she watched an older girl trying out all the different-coloured eye shadows on the back of her hand. A saleslady opened the jars for her, holding the painted hand up to the light where the colours gleamed and twinkled. Next came eyelashes, and these really fascinated Jennifer. They transformed this rather plain girl into a beauty. "These are our Chinese brushes for outlining the eyes," said the saleslady as she laid out ten beautiful bamboo brushes with bristles, some very thick, others delicately fine.

"May I help you?" Suddenly the saleslady turned to Jennifer.

"Oh, I was just looking," she stammered.

"Yes, dear, but you shouldn't stare, you know," the lady reprimanded, and Jennifer moved away.

It must be such fun to put all that make-up on your

face, she thought. Really very much like colouring a picture. Then she remembered what Danièlle had told her about ballet make-up for stage – it was hard to do. The idea was to make your eyes appear very large. In the old days ballet make-up looked very artificial, but now it had become more natural.

Through the confusing mass of people, Jennifer caught sight of Emily signalling to her from the other side of the room. She made her way across piled-up shoe boxes and outstretched stockinged feet to a counter stacked high with coloured leotards.

"These are on sale," said Mrs. Stock excitedly. "Is there anything here you girls fancy?" She held up a lacy red leotard.

Jennifer and Emily rummaged through the heap then looked at each other sadly – no black leotards and no pink tights. Jennifer fingered the tempting red leotard and pictured Miss Collins' horror if she ever dared to wear such an article of clothing to class.

Examining more of the store's magical contents, Emily raced over to a row of downy stoles in pink and green. "Just feel how soft they are!" she exclaimed, and as she spoke the feathers fluttered under her breath.

Jennifer was drawn to a case of tiaras. Crowns studded with twinkling jewels gleamed in the light. How magnificent it would be to wear one of those! "Are they real diamonds?" Jennifer asked the salesgirl.

"Oh, no, dear, they're glass," was the reply.

"Of course," said Jennifer hastily, but she knew that if she could ever wear one she would pretend that the jewels were priceless.

Mrs. Stock had ferreted out another room. "Girls," she called in her booming voice, "the bahlet stuff is in here."

Emily rushed over to join her mother, with Jennifer following more reluctantly. The room in which they now found themselves was quite ordinary. One wall was lined with shoe boxes and Jennifer smelled the special leathery odour that ballet slippers have. Another wall shelved countless boxes of pink tights and black leotards. Now they knew for certain that they were in the right place. Even more interesting to Jennifer was a corner where bags of every description were stacked higgeldy-piggeldy. Some were leather, some were plastic, some were canvas. Some had zippers, some had drawstrings and some had locks. They were of all colours, but most of all Jennifer's eyes were riveted to a sign with large red letters: REDUCED TO CLEAR.

Before Jennifer could investigate further, Mrs. Stock had already nabbed a young saleslady. "These ballerinas wish to purchase some stockings," she announced grandly.

Emily tugged at her mother's sleeve. "Mom, we can ask for what we want."

Jennifer quickly intercepted. In a grown-up, businesslike manner, she asked for pink tights.

"What size?" the salesgirl responded.

What an embarrassment! Neither of the girls knew so they were each given three pairs to try on. As they headed into a curtained cubbyhole, Mrs. Stock called after them, "Buy them plenty big so there's room for you to grow, girls. I can't believe the price of them."

I wonder how much they are? Jennifer worried. She tapped her purse. Altogether she had eleven dollars.

It was very awkward getting into these long-desired tights. They weren't as flexible as Jennifer had imagined and she kept losing her balance trying to wriggle one leg in while standing on the other. Finally Emily solved the problem by sitting down and pulling the tights onto both legs at once. To her dismay, they were so snug that she couldn't stand up. As for Jennifer, the smallest pair was so large that her knees bagged and the feet extended far past her own toes. Mrs. Stock came in with a larger size for Emily, and Jennifer peeled off the pink nylon and slipped out of the dressing room.

"How were they?" asked the salesgirl uninterestedly. The room had filled with demanding customers.

"A bit big."

"Well, they're the smallest we have," snapped the girl and started to fold them back into the bag.

"Oh, no, I'll take them," Jennifer said hastily, then, "How much are they?"

"Four ninety-five," said the girl over her shoulder, hurrying on to an impatient parent.

Jennifer calculated as fast as she could. That meant she would only have six dollars and five cents left. She eyed the heap of bags in the corner. Emily and her mother were still fussing in the dressing room and the salesgirl was occupied.

Ever so casually, Jennifer went over to the pile and picked up the price tag of a big blue bag. Twenty-five dollars, reduced to sixteen ninety-five. She dropped it quickly. That one was a real leather bag. She looked at another tag, then another, and another, until there was only one left. Dispiritedly, Jennifer checked it. Nine ninety-five. Oh, dear! But wait! There was a red line through that, and underneath in pencil "Reduced to $6.95." Jennifer blinked at the ticket, then she checked the bag. It was made of canary-yellow canvas with two compartments and a big flap but, best of all, it had a shoulder strap. This would be perfect, thought Jennifer who was always laden with things for ballet class as well as her school books. She slipped the strap over her shoulder and checking in the mirror, she approved of what she saw. She felt terribly grownup. She was using her fingers to figure the finances when she became aware of the salesgirl watching her, which instantly made her self-conscious. What was she going to do? After she had paid for one pair of tights she would have six dollars and five cents left. She needed another ninety cents.

Unexpectedly Mrs. Stock was beside her. "Oh, that's really smart, Jennifer. Expensive, I bet."

Jennifer explained her problem and Emily's mother clucked her tongue. "That bag is a bargain," she said. She thought for a minute. "Wait! You're in luck, young lady," she shouted. Jennifer stared at her, uncomprehending. Mrs. Stock dug into her large purse. "By walking here today we saved the bus fare I had put aside. So, don't you refuse now," her chubby fingers closed on the change, "it's all yours."

Jennifer hardly dared look down at her hand as Mrs. Stock triumphantly placed the money in it. Impetuously she grabbed Mrs. Stock's arm and gave it a huge squeeze. "Oh, thank you! I can't tell you how grateful I am!"

Knowing she practically owned it, Jennifer really inspected the bag now. And once Emily had found tights to fit, the three of them took their choices to the cash register. Mrs. Stock's purchases consisted of shiny green eye shadow and dark-red lipstick. "You shouldn't have taken so long," she teased.

The saleslady wrapped everything in silver plastic bags. But Jennifer asked that her bag not be wrapped, and she proudly offered to carry everyone's things in it.

"My goodness, it's late!" exclaimed Mrs. Stock as they finally stepped out of the shop. "We were in there for over two hours. Look, it's dark now. I don't know about you two, but I'm starving. What would you girls say about getting something to eat?"

Jennifer and Emily looked at each other and grinned. They thought it was a wonderful idea.

Chapter Eleven

*T*he weeks were slipping by and there was still no word as to who would dance in the Christmas performances. At first Jennifer had spent each day nervously anticipating an announcement, but time kept passing and nothing was said. At night she and Emily would discuss the situation in whispers. Like true friends, each of them insisted it would be the other, but they both agreed that if Miss Collins had anything to do with it, Maureen would likely be chosen.

Just as everyone had warned Jennifer, the school life was demanding, and she was still surprised at how tired she was each night. Some part of her body would ache from all the stretching and tugging in class, and she found to her own amazement that she wanted nothing more than to soak in a hot tub and then jump into bed. Her family would never have believed it! However, it wasn't even possible to rest until she had completed all her homework.

Occasionally Jennifer wondered if she really should have left home and come to this school so far away. Just as Jim and Sue had said, she missed them, with all their teasing, and she counted the days and hours in the two weeks from one Sunday to the next when, at five o'clock, she spoke to her whole family on the phone. Her mother was wonderful about writing and every other day Jennifer would receive a long chatty letter, illustrated with witty sketches, telling her about life in Sault Ste. Marie. Packages came too, filled with Jennifer's favourite cookies and knitted slippers.

Jennifer was not good at writing letters. She even tried to keep a diary during her flashlight hours so she could remember what to say when she wrote home. But she was mostly so tired from doing her lessons that she could not write one word more than she absolutely had to.

Winter had come to Toronto and Jennifer bundled up to go outside. She hated being cold and so did her muscles now that she was a dancer. She found that in the chilly weather she had to work even harder to loosen up. Right now she was attempting to get all the way down in the front and side splits. Danièlle had advised her to do as much stretching as she could while she was young because her muscles would tighten as she grew older. Neither Emily nor Maureen had any trouble with the stretching and loosening exercises, but Jennifer had to persevere in order to get her legs as high as theirs.

Christmas exams were coming up in all the school

subjects. Jennifer needed to carry more books back and forth from the residence so she could study, and her new yellow bag served her well. One day she was trudging back to school after a hasty lunch when she heard someone calling her.

"Jennifer! Jennifer!" Turning, she saw Danièlle on the other side of the street, running hard to catch up with her.

"I've been looking for you all day," her friend said breathlessly. "I have something to tell you."

"What is it?" Jennifer could already guess that the news was good because Danièlle's eyes were sparkling with excitement.

"Oh, Jen! I've been asked to join the Performing Company!" said Danièlle.

"What!" Jennifer shrieked. "That's fantastic! But why – I mean, how?"

Although Danièlle was a graduate student, everyone knew she would have to wait at least a year before a place became vacant in the company.

"Well," explained Danièlle, "I had a phone call this morning from Madame Rose."

Jennifer gasped. "She called you on the phone?"

"Yes. She told me there've been a lot of injuries among the dancers recently and that one girl in the Corps de Ballet is off for six months with a torn knee ligament. So she recommended me to the directors and they said, yes, I would do."

"I bet you couldn't believe it." Jennifer's voice was filled with awe.

"I'm glad I was sitting down," laughed Danièlle. "I

can't wait to call my parents tonight. And the best part of it is that I'll go on tour after Christmas, all over Canada."

Jennifer clapped her hands. "That's wonderful! Maybe my family will be able to see you then," she cried. "Oh, Danièlle, I'm so happy for you. When do you start?"

"I have rehearsals tomorrow and I've a lot to learn. But listen, I have to get fitted for pointe shoes tonight. Would you like to come with me?"

Jennifer looked at Danièlle incredulously. Would she like to come! She couldn't believe she was hearing such a thrilling question.

That evening Danièlle and Jennifer left the Student House after dinner. Mrs. Peers approved of Danièlle so there was no problem about getting permission, and off the two of them went to Smith's Theatrical Supplies. All the way there Jennifer badgered Danièlle with questions about toe shoes.

"They're called *pointe* shoes," Danièlle insisted, refusing to answer until Jennifer used the correct term.

"Oops, sorry," said Jennifer. "But tell me, what are they really made of? Is it true they have a wooden block so you can stand on your toes?"

"Absolutely not," said Danièlle, quite disgusted. "A pointe shoe is made of several layers of canvas that are stiffened and hardened in the toe with glue and shellac."

"That's all?" Jennifer was somewhat disappointed.

"That's all," confirmed Danièlle. "On top of the canvas the pink satin is stretched and this gives the shoe a delicate look. The sole is made of a thin flexible material

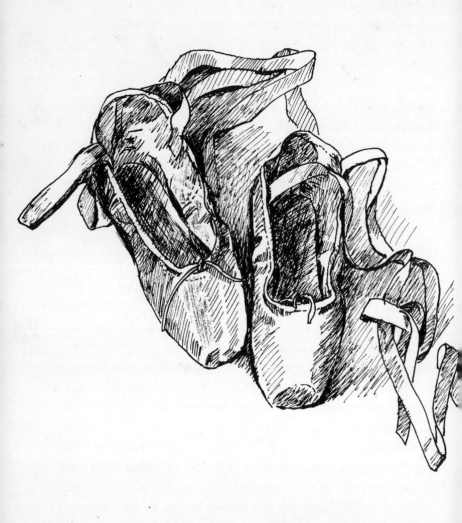

which gets softer as the heat of your foot moulds the shoe."

"You mean the shoes melt?"

"Exactly," smiled Danièlle. "They get very soft."

"How long does a pair of pointe shoes last?" asked Jennifer.

"Now that I'll be dancing seven and eight hours a day instead of just two as I did in class," said Danièlle, "I'll be using at least two to three pairs a week."

"But if they wear out so quickly, what keeps you up on your toes?"

"Ah," said Danièlle, "your own strength. The muscles in your toes, your arches, your ankles and all the way up your legs to your stomach. That's what you're training for now and that's why you won't be ready for pointe work for another year."

Jennifer shook her head. Everything in ballet was so much more complicated than she ever expected.

Danièlle and Jennifer arrived at Smith's and now its window was brightly lit with Christmas lights. The two girls went directly to the ballet department. The saleslady knew Danièlle by name and immediately brought out at least a dozen boxes of pointe shoes in her size.

Then began the tugging and pushing, testing and poking. Jennifer couldn't quite believe what was happening. How could Danièlle expect to get into such tiny shoes? It was like a scene out of *Cinderella*! And yet, with perseverance, she managed. They were all marked size four but Danièlle explained that each pair was different since they were made by hand. It wasn't enough just to get them on, though; Danièlle would hop up and down and walk around on her toes, testing, checking and comparing, never completely satisfied.

"Sorry, Jennifer," she said, "but it's essential that my shoes fit correctly or I won't be able to dance well. The last two pairs I had gave me blisters on my big toe so I have to be careful."

"Does it hurt to stand on your toes like that?" Jennifer asked. She would have loved to try one of the shoes herself.

"Yes and no," said Danièlle. "You get used to it." She held up another pair of shoes to her critical eye. "You must be sure they fit," she repeated, and she discharged this pair without even trying them on. "Those heel measurements were far too low. Sometimes you can just tell by the look of them how they'll be."

Six pairs of pointe shoes finally passed the stiff examination. Danièlle was at last satisfied that she had found what she wanted. She had tried on thirty-three pairs of shoes. Jennifer had counted. What would happen to the other pairs?

"Hopefully they'll be all right for someone else," said the saleslady, but she didn't seem too upset. It was obvious that this happened all the time when professional dancers came to pick their shoes. Jennifer was very proud to be accompanying Danièlle, who was almost in the company now. She herself still had to wait a whole year before she could buy her own pointe shoes. But from the sight of Danièlle's scarred and bandaged toes, Jennifer began to realize that dancing in pointe shoes wasn't going to be all fun. She had watched some of the classes ahead of her doing their very slow pointe exercises, and it occurred to her now that real pain may actually be involved. If people only knew how true it was when they said that dancing was a hard life!

It was late by the time Jennifer got back to the house. She said good night to Danièlle then slowly climbed the stairs. There was lots of homework to do and Jennifer suddenly remembered that she had a history test the next day. Oh dear, as usual she had left all her studying to the last minute.

Halfway up the stairs she paused. She was sure she heard someone crying. It's probably Suzanne, she thought. Suzanne bawled every night, no matter how Emily and Jennifer tried to cheer her up. There was a rumour around that she might not come back after Christmas since she couldn't adjust to living away from home. But as Jennifer neared the top she became uneasy. Reaching the door to her room, she realized that it wasn't Suzanne she was hearing. She hesitated a moment, then quietly went in.

Hunched in a tight little ball on her bed was Emily. When she looked up and saw Jennifer, her face contorted and she wailed even louder. Jennifer didn't know what to do or say. She had a premonition of what may be the matter and for one awful moment she wanted to run from the scene. But she rushed over to her friend.

"Oh, Emily, please don't cry," she pleaded, putting her hand on the girl's trembling shoulders. "What's wrong? Please tell me."

"It's you!" cried Emily. "It's you! They've chosen you!

You're going to perform with the company at Christmas." And she broke into choking sobs.

Here was the news Jennifer had been waiting to hear for weeks. She had thought she would be the happiest person in the world if this dream came true, and now she felt miserable and guilty. What could she say to comfort Emily?

"How did you find out?" Jennifer asked. "Maybe it's not true." She suppressed the eager questions that flooded into her mind.

"Oh, it's true," Emily replied bitterly. "I heard Mrs. Peers talking to Miss Blake on the phone. She was saying she couldn't figure out why the ballet teachers had chosen you."

Jennifer fumed. Wasn't this a ballet school? What did Mrs. Peers know? Anyway, it was none of her business.

Emily sniffed, trying to stop her tears. "Oh, I'm sorry, Jennifer. I shouldn't have told you that part."

"It's okay," Jennifer said quickly. "It's true. You deserve to be chosen just as much as I do. I'd do anything to make you happy again." For a moment she convinced herself that she wouldn't mind giving up her part. Then she said, "If only it could have been the two of us. But wait, who's the other girl, then?"

"You'll never guess."

"Maureen," Jennifer said flatly.

"Yes," Emily replied. "I heard Mrs. Peers go on and on about how talented she is and how they have to keep her interested." And of course, don't forget, she's thin," Emily added resentfully.

Jennifer tried to talk about other things, but some-how the forbidden subject kept coming back into their conversation. She wanted to cheer Emily up.

"It will probably turn out to be hard work and not that much fun," she said. Then it occurred to Jennifer that she wouldn't be able to go home for Christmas. This was a blow and something that in all her weeks of dreaming she hadn't contemplated.

"But you wanted this chance more than anything else in the world, didn't you?" Emily asked.

Jennifer nodded rather doubtfully.

* * *

Next day Jennifer entered the school to find a large crowd of students milling round the notice board.

"Well," Maureen said as she walked away, "I suppose we are just about the same height."

Jennifer stood looking at the list of chosen students for a long, long time. Some classmates were congratulat-ing her but others said nothing.

This was the moment Jennifer had been waiting for. She had pictured it in her dreams a thousand times in the last few weeks; yet now she found that she couldn't be happy without being sad.

Chapter Twelve

*I*t took Jennifer a day or two to break the good news to her family. She needed to be alone to organize her thoughts, and Mrs. Peers was becoming even more of a problem. Saturday morning she managed to sneak down to the cellar and write the letter that was burning a hole in her head.

Dear Mum and Dad, Jim and Sue,
How are you? I am fine, and Danièlle is too. Guess what? I am going to be in a real ballet! I have been chosen to dance on stage as an extra with the Performing Company. I'm so excited. I'll be wearing make-up and a costume just like the professionals. I was chosen with Maureen, the girl in my class who is really good. I wonder who chose me? Emily is *very* disappointed and I'm upset about that. It would have

been so much fun if it could have been us two. Madame Rose says there will be shows on Christmas Eve and Boxing Day, which means I won't be able to come home for Christmas. I'm really sorry but you do understand, don't you?

I miss you all – so much.

Love,
Jennifer.

When she finished the letter, she felt far more homesick than before. Jennifer was lonely these days. She missed Danièlle whom she hadn't seen since she joined the Performing Company weeks ago. Danièlle had a knack for saying just the right thing to make Jennifer forget her troubles, and it made her feel proud to have her as a friend. She often boasted about what a good dancer Danièlle was and how well she was doing in the Performing Company, but she'd noticed some of the students becoming annoyed with her. Yesterday Maureen had said, "How can you know? You haven't seen her working recently. I've heard she's having trouble remembering her parts in the different ballets."

This put a stop to Jennifer's boasting. Come to think of it, Danièlle kept promising that Jennifer could come and watch her rehearse, but she had never actually invited her. Jennifer was troubled. If Danièlle was finding it difficult, maybe she too would have problems learning her part in the Christmas performances. The more she mulled over it, the more nervous she became. She wished she knew what she'd have to do so that she could think about it and practise.

One day Jennifer dared to ask Miss Collins about it as they passed in the hall.

She seemed annoyed at the question.

"Don't be in such a hurry, Jennifer," she said. "You have three and a half weeks, and you'll be shown your steps in plenty of time. They won't be rehearsing *Cinderella* until just before the season opens."

"*Cinderella!*" Jennifer gasped. "Am I going to dance in *Cinderella?*"

"Why yes, didn't you know?" answered Miss Collins, her eyes flicking to her watch. "You and Maureen will be Cinderella's attendants at the ball."

Jennifer couldn't trust herself to say anything. She just stood there, silent and bursting, as Miss Collins hurried away to cope with her daily emergencies.

Jennifer's ballet lesson that day was an hour of sheer joy. She was so excited at the prospect of dancing in *Cinderella*, her favourite ballet, that she was ready to tackle anything in class. As she worked, she cherished the image of Miss Brook, the professional dancer, and she pretended that her inspiration stood before her once again. Jennifer didn't despair when Mr. Young gave them a difficult combination. She found that with her spirits lifted, the movements flowed more easily. It was too bad she couldn't be in a good mood every day. And Jennifer let go of the barre without a quiver.

Mr. Young noticed her radiance and commented on her smile. "Jennifer, you look great," he exclaimed. "That's what I want to see, class. Less self-consciousness. Remember, it's part of your training to learn how to look pleasant. It's one of the most important qualities a dancer has while performing on stage. You're all teaching your bodies to be beautiful, but the beauty must also come from within."

Jennifer listened intently. It's true, she agreed. She looked at Maureen who was undeniably beautiful, but then she glanced over at Suzanne. She was not a pretty girl. She had a very plain face, but when she danced her expression changed and Jennifer would be amazed at how really lovely she was.

At the end of class Mr. Young asked Jennifer to stay behind. He wanted to give her some special corrections for her jumps. This was a sign that she had done well and Jennifer was eager for his extra help. He tapped her leg. "You're not really stretching the back of that knee," he said. "And your left foot isn't pointing. Try again."

Jennifer jumped and jumped, trying as hard as she could to correct her faults.

"Try again."

But it was hard to satisfy Mr. Young.

"Again."

Finally her teacher nodded. "Good girl. You've got it now. But when you jump you mustn't take your mind off that left foot of yours for a second. It's flapping and that's a bad habit of yours."

Jennifer nodded in agreement. Why, she wondered, was she always so stricken for words with her ballet teachers?

Mr. Young gave her one of his funny winks and patted her on the head. "Keep it up, kid," he said. "Well, that's enough for today. Boy, could I use a cup of coffee!" And he hurried out of the studio.

Jennifer watched him go, then turned and looked at herself in the mirror. Was that really her standing there, Jennifer Allen, ten years old, training to be a ballet dancer? That girl looked so funny with her brown hair pulled tightly back, her skinny legs and baggy knees and feet too large for the rest of her. She raised her arms; so did the mirror. She blinked her eyes; so did the mirror. She smiled; and the strange, funny girl grinned back at her.

"Well, Jennifer," her image in the mirror said, "enough of this dawdling. Let's get to work." And she practised jumping the way Mr. Young had insisted. Soon she was breathing in short, wheezy puffs. "Wow!" she gasped, laughing at her conspirator in the glass. "It's really hard that way, isn't it?"

"Who are you talking to?" a voice asked.

This time Jennifer really jumped. She turned around to see a boy named Peter standing in the doorway staring at her.

"Oh, was I talking?" Jennifer replied, furious with herself for blushing. "I was trying to keep my knees straight in *jetés*, the way Mr. Young wants. But it hardly seems possible. Watch." Jennifer tried a couple more jumps. She stopped again, out of breath. "There doesn't seem time. No sooner am I in the air than I'm down again."

Peter nodded. "I know exactly what you mean. There's so much to think about in that split-second when you're in the air. Hey! Let me try something." He grabbed Jennifer by the waist. "Let me lift you when

you jump," he said. "I've watched the boys do it in pas de deux classes."

Before she could protest Jennifer found herself in the air. Now she had lots of time to straighten her knees. She could even stretch both feet. She felt wonderful, as if she were flying, until *thud!* she landed loudly.

"We have to time this together," Peter said. "The secret of the girl appearing as light as a feather is just a matter of coordination between her and her partner." Jennifer looked at him. "I have to lift you just as you take off," he continued, "and you have to really jump."

They tried it again. Her eyes flickered over to the mirror and Jennifer couldn't believe the sight of herself suspended in the air. "This is fun!" she cried.

"Yeah," said Peter, not quite as sure. "I think I'm going to have to start doing more pushups though." He ruefully rubbed his arms. "This time, jump straight up and don't let your back drop," he said as he prepared to lift again.

Up she went – Jennifer Allen, the ballerina. Enamoured with the sight of herself in the mirror, she gaily flapped her arms like a swan queen. Suddenly Peter fumbled. He had lost his grip and down Jennifer came with a sickening crash. She felt her left ankle twist horribly and a stab of pain shot through it as she fell to the floor. An echo of silence, then Peter reached for her in alarm.

"Oh, Jennifer, are you all right? When you waved your arms like that I couldn't hold on. I'm so sorry."

"I'm fine," said Jennifer bravely, but she bit her lip hard to keep from crying. Her ankle hurt badly. "Could you help me up?" Gingerly she stood but at the first step her left foot crumbled under her weight. The pain was sharp like a knife. With Peter's help Jennifer hopped out of the studio. She couldn't believe it. One minute she had been so happy, now she was in agonizing pain. It had all happened so quickly.

Out in the hall they were immediately surrounded. Peter impatiently fended off all the questions. Finally someone managed to fetch Miss Harris, the school nurse.

Amid all the fuss, Jennifer sat quietly on the floor. Huge tears rolled down her face, even though she thought she wasn't crying. She heard words like "doctor," "hospital" and "x-rays" as if in a dream. She saw Miss Harris' grim face through wet lashes and a mist of deep misery. Jennifer could think of one thing only. It was three and a half weeks until the Christmas performances. Was she going to be able to dance in *Cinderella*?

Chapter Thirteen

*U*pon arrival at the hospital Jennifer was sent to the x-ray department. She had to sit up on a big, black table while a man twisted her foot into excruciating positions.

"Oh, ow," Jennifer stammered in pain whenever her foot was moved, but the grim man never looked at her. It was just another left ankle he was dealing with.

"Hold it," he'd command while the machine whirred and the table shook.

Next Jennifer was taken to a curtained cubbyhole with a cot in it. "Wait here," the nurse said, and she closed the cotton drapes, leaving Jennifer alone. There was nothing to do but sit and listen to doctors' questions and patients' answers from the other cubicles. Somewhere a man was moaning in pain.

A while later the nurse returned with an ice pack for

Jennifer's foot which was now so swollen that the ankle bone had completely disappeared. The cold intensified the pain to such a degree that Jennifer removed the pack, replacing it whenever she heard footsteps outside.

Two hours later the curtains were drawn back. A young man dressed all in white gave her a wide smile. "Hi! I'm Dr. Sing." He shook her hand. "What's the trouble?" Jennifer told him. "Oh well, we must take special care of you!" he exclaimed. "You're looking at a real ballet fan, so I know how essential it is that your foot heal properly. Let's have a look at it."

Jennifer gripped the sides of the cot as the doctor examined her foot. The pain was unbearable every time he touched it.

"Well, you've got a sprain of this ligament here," he finally spoke. Jennifer winced as he poked at the puffy mass at the side of her foot. "You may even have torn some of the fibres."

"How long will it take to get better?" Jennifer asked, trying to conceal her impatience. Her voice quavered. "You see, I've been chosen to dance with the Performing Company in *Cinderella*." She stopped. Her eyes were filling again.

"Well," hesitated Dr. Sing, "it's hard to predict these things. An injury like this could take three weeks or so." He looked at her anguished face. "You must remember, if you dance on that foot before it's completely better, you're in danger of permanently weakening the ligament. However, your age is in your favour. I want you to have ten days of complete rest and then come back to see me."

"Ten days," Jennifer echoed sadly.

"Yes," said Dr. Sing. "And remember, no dancing at all! You must give that ligament every chance to heal."

When Jennifer finally returned to the Student House, Peter was waiting anxiously for her on the steps outside. She had been at the hospital for three and a half hours and for him the suspense had been unbearable. He was relieved to learn that no bones were broken, for he felt guilty about the accident even though Jennifer insisted it had been her fault. "It was so foolish of me that I was even embarrassed to tell the doctor how it had happened." She gave a rueful laugh.

"Well, if you're daring enough to let me lift you again, I'll piggy-back you wherever you need to go for the next few days," Peter offered, and Jennifer giggled this time.

Everyone in the Student House swarmed around the injured girl when she went inside and Jennifer had to repeat her hospital story many times. Mrs. Peers was surprisingly soothing, not nearly as frantic now that something was really wrong. She had a room prepared on the main floor since Jennifer would be unable to climb the stairs, and Emily had carried down all her things. Everyone was so sympathetic that the leaden lump inside Jennifer felt as if it would soon burst.

At last she was alone in her strange new room. In the dark Jennifer tried to figure out what had happened to her, and why. And she let the tears flow freely for the first time since her accident. Her swollen foot would not let her sleep; its throbbing would not let her forget. Dr. Sing had strapped it very tightly with yards of sticky white bandage that went all the way up her leg to her knee. At first the support had felt necessary and comforting, but now the tightness was intolerable and Jennifer longed to rip the tape off. Her toes were numb and cold, yet when she tried to wiggle them her ankle would stab with pain. Hours passed. Jennifer grew tired of crying and she realized how exhausted she was. She slipped into sleep, hoping that her dreams would dissolve the nightmare of her day.

* * *

For the next ten days, Jennifer learned first-hand what it was like to be an injured dancer. All her life she had taken for granted that she could run and skip and jump; now she could barely walk. Her limp made her very self-conscious; and it took her so long to get from one place to another that she lost many a battle against the angry tears of frustration. Without dancing, she felt empty; yet her mind was filled with miserable thoughts. Jennifer felt left out and worthless, almost ashamed of herself because she was disabled.

It was like a form of punishment to sit and watch the ballet classes, yet Danièlle had insisted that Jennifer do it. "You can learn so much from watching others. This injury could be a good thing for you, Miss Impatience," she'd said, and in spite of a wretched few days Jennifer began to find it intriguing to watch. She would marvel at her classmates' movements, sure that such difficult steps were beyond her powers. Yet she became so perceptive that she could also pick out mistakes just as quickly as Miss Collins could. She began to understand why the teachers insisted on such perfection. Jennifer imagined herself as an audience and she became very demanding indeed.

Yet there were times when the power of the music was irresistible and Jennifer found it impossible to sit still. She would attempt to stretch her foot, only to be greeted with a sickening stab of pain.

Mr. Young noticed her restlessness as she watched his class. "You don't have to waste your time, my little friend," he said. "If you do twice the number of stomach exercises and stretches lying on the floor, you'll find that you'll be stronger than ever to cope with that floppy foot of yours."

He was right, and Jennifer knew it, but floor exercises were the part of ballet that she liked the least!

Miss Collins also had plans to keep Jennifer occupied. One day she sat her on a tall stool in front of the mirror.

"This is an excellent opportunity for you to work on the form of your head and arms," she said. For over an hour she made Jennifer tilt, incline, roll and turn her head. At the same time she guided her arms through their five positions. "Think of holding a basket of flowers," Miss Collins said at one point. "There. Now you have the right curve without letting your elbows jut out." Miss Collins also explained that one arm should relate to the other. "If you can see in your mind a piece of elastic attached to the middle finger of each hand, you will always be able to draw an imaginary line with your arms. This is extremely important in ballet."

Jennifer nodded, squinting at the glass. From watching classes, she understood what Miss Collins wanted.

She had seen that Maureen's work had a natural flow, while other students made stiff or jerky motions.

"If you continue conscientiously with what I've shown you, you'll be a better dancer after your injury," said Miss Collins, and she gave Jennifer one of her rare smiles.

After Miss Collins left, Jennifer remained seated on the stool and stared at herself in the mirror. Although she was grateful to her teacher, she was glad the lesson was over. Her arms were tired and aching, and her foot throbbed from hanging from the high stool. She found it so hard to have to smile and act as if nothing were bothering her. No one, Jennifer fretted, really understood how much she was suffering. Sitting there in her school clothes, she didn't look or feel like a dancer anymore. She felt as if these days of immobility had turned her body into a lump of lead.

And she was deeply disturbed by what Maureen had said to Emily in the dressing room before lunch. "Is Jennifer going to be all right for *Cinderella?*"

"Of course," her friend had replied.

"Well, I just thought," continued Maureen," that if she isn't better soon, they might choose someone else."

There had been silence and Jennifer hobbled out as fast as she could. She had never felt so alone or so unsure of what she was doing. She longed to flee home to her family but she hadn't even told them about her accident. She had planned to write as soon as she was better. Now it seemed almost impossible that her ankle could stop hurting in time for the Christmas performances.

She wriggled down from the stool and made her way

over to the mirror. "Jennifer Allen," she asked herself, "are you really sure that ballet dancing is for you?"

After a long, long while, her reflection nodded in silence.

Chapter Fourteen

*D*r. Sing stopped by a few days later to find out how Jennifer was progressing. He had been very touched by the sad girl who so much wanted to dance.

"You have the same kind of dedication that we need in medicine," he told her.

A week had passed since the accident and the severe pain had diminished. He found Jennifer walking more easily. They sat on the stone steps for a chat.

"Are you also a newcomer to Canada?" the young doctor asked.

"Oh, no," she replied. "I've lived here for two years."

"Me too," he laughed. "I came from Hong Kong eighteen months ago. But of course I had a few more problems with the language than you did. Tell me about England."

That weekend he invited Jennifer, Emily and Peter to a Chinese restaurant. It was a special place where the chef didn't speak English and Dr. Sing ordered without even consulting the menu. They couldn't believe their eyes when heaping plates of duck, lobster and rice were carried steaming from the kitchen. The three children tried to follow Dr. Sing's instructions on the use of chopsticks, but they all gave up when the aroma from their plates became too tempting.

"This sure beats Mrs. Peers' cooking," remarked Peter, and Jennifer readily agreed. It was her first taste of Oriental food and this time she knew she would have no trouble remembering every juicy detail in her next letter home. That reminded her, it had been over a week since she'd written. It occurred to Jennifer that Mrs. Beauchamp might hear of her injury and inform her parents before she did, and she suddenly felt guilty. If only she could put it off a little longer until she was dancing again; otherwise her mother would surely persuade her to come home for Christmas.

Dr. Sing, Peter and Emily were busily chatting about ballet.

"Classical dance is one of my country's most revered treasures. We have traditional dances that have been handed down for generations, for hundreds of years," the young man said with pride.

Peter nodded. He had read a great deal about China. "Isn't there a drum dance that you must train for years to do properly?" he asked.

"Oh, yes," Dr. Sing nodded, smiling. "Just like your ballet which in its beauty looks deceptively simple. Last

year I saw a performance of *The Sleeping Beauty* that took my breath away."

"Oh, that's the ballet where the ballerina has to balance on her pointe on one leg for ages!" said Emily excitedly. "I've seen that one too."

"Yes, the part you've described is the famous Rose Adagio, one of the most challenging tests in classical ballet. And, Peter, let me tell you about the Prince's marvellous solo in the last act – he does a circle of double turns in the air –"

Lately the ballet talk at the school had left Jennifer despondent. But Dr. Sing's eager voice conjured up all the magic and excitement that she had experienced at her first ballet performance. She wanted to leap up from the table; she was filled with inspiration again. And whenever Jennifer was really happy, the only way to completely express what she felt was to dance. But her foot reminded her of reality and she fingered the fraying bandage.

Why, oh why, did it have to happen? Why me, why me? she asked herself for the thousandth time.

As though sensing Jennifer's thoughts, Dr. Sing turned to her. "We'll see you Tuesday, Jennifer, and we'll have a look at that ankle of yours."

Jennifer nodded, her troubled eyes searching Dr. Sing's face.

"Something you should realize about a career in dancing, Jennifer, is that injuries are a part of it," Dr. Sing warned gently. "You dancers are superb athletes but you still push your bodies too hard."

"What about when we're more experienced?" asked Peter guiltily.

"I'm afraid that as long as you dance you will never be free from the possibility of injury. Your bodies are not machines and even they break down at some time. In your lives there'll be high points and low points. But," Dr. Sing added brightly, "you'll also be the most physically fit people I know. How about some fortune cookies?" he grinned. "They can tell the future better than I can."

* * *

Tuesday came, not nearly as quickly as Jennifer might have wished. All weekend she had worried about what Dr. Sing's verdict would be. Was he going to let her go back to dancing? Time seemed to be passing so quickly. The first *Cinderella* performance was now only two weeks and three days away.

Just this morning Miss Collins had stopped Jennifer in the hall to ask her how her foot was feeling. "You know, if you're not back in class this week," she said worriedly, "we'll have to get a replacement for you."

Dancing in *Cinderella* meant everything to Jennifer. Was this dream going to be taken away from her?

"I'm going to see Dr. Sing at twelve o'clock," Jennifer blurted out, her eyes imploring Miss Collins.

"Come and see me when you get back from the hospital," Miss Collins said.

Three hours later Jennifer sat uneasily on the narrow examining table in a white hospital room. She had been waiting a long time. The clock on the wall indicated five minutes past one. Perhaps Dr. Sing had forgotten all about her, she brooded. Jennifer was fascinated by a tray of instruments beside her. She surveyed the different silver shapes. What were they used for? she wondered. Just as she reached over for a magnifying glass, Dr. Sing came dashing in.

"Sorry I'm late, Jennifer," he apologized, pulling a mask off his face. He went over to the sink to scrub his hands. "Well, how has that ankle of yours been behaving?"

He proceeded to cut through the sticky layers of tape until Jennifer's pale and wrinkled foot was exposed. It looked shrivelled next to the healthy one beside it. Under the doctor's gentle probing, Jennifer rotated her ankle, first one way and then the other. She was relieved to see most of the swelling was gone.

"Does it hurt to do that?" he asked.

"Well, it's a bit stiff and sore," she admitted.

"Stand up," said Dr. Sing. "Let's see you put your weight on it."

Jennifer cautiously obeyed. There were no stabs but her ankle felt wobbly without its strapping.

"Raise your foot and try stretching it," Dr. Sing said.

Carefully Jennifer arched her instep, encouraged when it moved without resistance. Next, using the table as a barre, she attempted a plié. She was unable to push all the way down without the familiar pain. She looked at Dr. Sing in alarm.

"The ankle is protecting itself with stiffness," he said.

Jennifer watched Dr. Sing as he wrote illegible notes in her file.

"Basically, the ligament has healed," he said at last.

"But, as you can feel yourself, that foot is not completely better. If you promise to be sensible, you can probably work through this. You may start your ballet lessons again, but you must take it very easy and I want no jumping for at least ten days. Now listen, Jennifer," he said earnestly, "your greatest danger is trying to get back into shape too fast and twisting the ankle again while it's still unstable. Then it would take twice as long to get better and you could end up with a chronic injury which could jeopardize your whole dancing career."

"Dr. Sing," Jennifer asked timidly, "what about *Cinderella*? Will I be able to dance with the Performing Company?"

"When is that supposed to be?" he asked.

"In two weeks and three days," said Jennifer.

"Well –" Dr. Sing pondered. "I really can't say for sure. It will just be up to you and how quickly you can strengthen that foot without forcing it. Also, you have to get the rest of your body back into shape. I'm sure there will be other chances in the future. If you miss this one, it won't be the end of the world."

He smiled with sympathy at Jennifer's agonized expression. "But maybe I'll take a chance on a ticket. What date should I buy it for?"

Jennifer beamed. "The twentieth of December, Dr. Sing!"

* * *

Jennifer hesitated outside Miss Collins' door. She had never visited the assistant principal's office before but she had seen many students coming and going, in smiles and in tears. Taking a deep breath she tapped on the door. Not even Jennifer heard that! She knocked again.

"Come in," Miss Collins called, and Jennifer obeyed. She stood watching Miss Collins who was busy writing at her desk.

"Yes?" she said without looking up.

"Er, you asked me to tell you what Dr. Sing said."

"Oh, yes." Miss Collins looked up and Jennifer was surprised to see that she had glasses on. Her teacher looked very tired.

"He says it's getting better and that I can start back slowly –"

"What about the performances of *Cinderella?*" Miss Collins interrupted. "Can we count on you for them?"

"I think so," Jennifer said without conviction. Her foot was throbbing from all its new activity of the day.

"Oh, but I have to know," Miss Collins insisted. She leafed through sheets of paper till she found the one she was looking for. "Let me see, I had an understudy picked out. Yes – Kathy Tobins . . . I think, Jennifer, that we'll have her cover the rehearsals just in case you aren't able to dance in time. How long did the doctor think it would take?"

"He didn't say, Miss Collins, but he's going to buy a ticket," answered Jennifer.

"I'm delighted to hear it," replied Miss Collins as she went back to her work. "Thank you, dear." And Jennifer was dismissed.

Chapter Fifteen

Christmas was not far off and each day the postman's load grew larger. Since the beginning of the school year, Jennifer and Emily had competed to see who received the most mail, and now Emily was taking the lead. Every day the two girls would race each other home from school.

"Oh boy, another package!" Emily exclaimed one afternoon. "That's the third one this week."

Jennifer was silent as she leafed through the stack of letters. She'd heard nothing from home since her telephone conversation last Sunday. Madame Beauchamp had lived up to her reputation and her family had found out about her injury.

"Why didn't you tell us, Jenny! Are you all right?" her mother asked her over and over again. "Do you want me to come and take care of you?"

127

Jennifer had hesitated. "No, Mum. I'm fine, really."

"Are you sure, Jenny? I'll come if you need me."

How hard it had been for Jennifer not to break down. She longed to see her mother, but not if it meant missing the Christmas show. Yet she was nagged by doubt as to whether she would be able to dance at all. Some days her ankle felt almost well again. Encouraged, Jennifer would eagerly attempt to catch up for lost time; then, when she least expected it, the foot would collapse under her weight, bringing back the razor-sharp stabs. Still, she was determined to participate in her ballet classes and she struggled to keep up with the others.

On her fifth day back to classes, she managed almost all of the exercises at the barre. But that night her ankle puffed in protest.

"You must try to keep the swelling down," said Emily. "Let me make an ice pack for you."

"Thanks," Jennifer murmured as she rubbed her aching foot.

It had been very quiet in their room that evening. Suzanne was packing to go home for good, and Emily was preparing her things to go to Edmonton for Christmas. Since that night when she had cried so bitterly, the subject of the performance had been avoided; and in her guilt Jennifer never said anything about their not going to Sault Ste. Marie for Christmas, as they had planned.

Emily stood by the dresser wrapping ice cubes in a towel. "I heard some rumours today," she said.

"Oh?" Something in her voice made Jennifer look up quickly.

"I know you have an understudy and it's not me."

Emily's words tumbled out. "I was upset at first but I'm not now. Oh, Jennifer, I hope you make it!"

* * *

As the days moved on, Jennifer inched her way back into condition. She found herself thinking less about her foot, which was a sign that it was getting better, and she was regaining some of her strength. She still faltered when jumping on the weaker leg. And whenever she wobbled, she felt as if Maureen and Kathy Tobins were watching her.

But Miss Collins had some encouraging words. "Here's a student, class, who has used a setback to her advantage. She's continued to develop her technique. Jennifer, your line and form have definitely improved."

Emily too would point out the steps that Jennifer could do better each day.

To everyone, including Miss Collins, Jennifer pretended that her ankle no longer hurt. She was nervous of their watchful eyes. She had to convince them that she was well enough to dance in the forthcoming performances, even though she wasn't sure herself.

This was the first year that Jennifer had done her own Christmas shopping. Her present for Emily had been wrapped and ready for many days. On the night before Emily was going home to Edmonton, the two girls ceremoniously exchanged their gifts. Jennifer gave her friend an illustrated dictionary of ballet, a book she herself very much wanted. She'd even found a photo of Madame Rose in it.

Emily handed Jennifer a small, square box tied with a tinsel bow. Jennifer read the note on the card:

Merry Christmas, Jennifer. Good luck in your performances. I'll be thinking of you.
Love,
Emily.

"Oh, thank you," Jennifer said gaily. "I must confess I'm quite excited now that it looks like I'll be ready. I shall write you and describe every exciting detail of what happens backstage, and —"

Jennifer paused. She noticed that Emily was avoiding her eyes. Now that she thought about it, her friend had been tense ever since . . . Could it be that she was still upset even though she had so firmly denied it?

"I'm sure it will be you next time," Jennifer consoled.

"No, Jennifer," Emily replied softly, "it will never be me."

Chapter Sixteen

*T*he next day Miss Collins called Jennifer and Maureen to her office.

"You're to report to the Grand Theatre at three o'clock," she told them. "Oh, and don't forget to tell Kathy."

When the girls arrived they were met by the ballet mistress who led them into a studio apart from the company dancers. This disappointed Jennifer, who had been hoping she would see Danièlle. The short, stocky woman very carefully explained what they would be required to do in the performance.

Jennifer was amazed at how she knew everybody's part in the ballet. Maureen and Jennifer were the two smallest, so they had been selected as fairy attendants at the Grand Ball in the second act. This meant they were to carry Cinderella's train and follow her everywhere.

"You must never leave her side," said the ballet mistress, "except of course when Cinderella dances her solos and pas de deux."

Jennifer and Maureen looked at each other. How would they know when the time came?

"Later, when the clock commences its midnight chimes, you do a little dance of fright and then dash off the stage on the twelfth stroke. Now watch closely, this is how you begin."

The steps of the choreography were not difficult. After all her worrying, Jennifer had little trouble learning the movements. However, she found it necessary to favour her right foot when pushing off for certain jumps. She was constantly aware of the tall, slim Kathy who was working hard right in a line with her and at times in front. The ballet mistress seemed to have taken a liking to her, and Jennifer grew more anxious each time Kathy was given a correction. Did the mistress know that Kathy was just the understudy? Somebody should tell her! Jennifer brooded.

When the ballet mistress took a five-minute coffee break, the three girls huddled in a corner trying to piece the steps together.

"What comes after the single pirouette to the left?" whispered Maureen.

"Is it jump, step run, jump?" said Kathy after deliberating a minute.

"Yes, that's it," joined in Jennifer. "I think it goes like this."

It took two hours to satisfy the ballet mistress that the students knew their parts and even then Jennifer was disappointed that her first rehearsal was over so soon. It was much more fun to dance for a story than for an exercise.

"Thank you, girls" said the ballet mistress. "You'll have a chance to go over everything at rehearsal next week. But I do hope you'll think about your steps in the meantime."

Jennifer smiled. She knew she wasn't going to be able to think of anything else.

"The next thing you must do is go upstairs to the wardrobe department," the lady said. "This theatre is large and the backstage area has many corridors that can lead you astray. I'm afraid I don't have time to take you myself but I'll draw a map." She gave the directions to Kathy who consulted the scrap of paper.

"It's on the sixth floor," she announced to the others. "Follow me."

Saying goodbye to the ballet mistress, the three girls set off down a passageway in search of the circular staircase. After many minutes of lifting tired feet, the newcomers found themselves outside a bubbly glass door on which WARDROBE was painted in large black letters. The last one up the stairs, Jennifer was troubled that Kathy had come here with them. Was she going to have a costume made as well?

The climb had been well worth it, for once they opened the door the three girls found themselves in a place even more wonderful than Smith's Theatrical Supplies. Magnificent costumes filled every square inch of space. There were so many that some were hung on

racks from the ceiling. Gowns of gleaming satin and capes of rich velvet spilled from above.

Mesmerized, Jennifer didn't notice Maureen and Kathy going through another door which led into the workroom.

"Are you the extras?" she heard a voice call out. Jennifer hurried in after them.

The hum and drone of sewing machines enveloped heads that never looked up from their measuring, pinning and snipping. A tubby lady finally rose from one of the tables where she had been cutting a great mass of material. She checked a list tacked up on the wall.

"Let's see," she said. "Allen and Anderson?"

"Yes," the two girls answered proudly, and Jennifer's eyes darted exaltingly over to Kathy Tobins' face.

"My, you two are tiny!" the wardrobe mistress exclaimed as she reached for their costumes. "I guess we've a bit of stitching to do to make these fit properly."

The dresses were beautiful. They had lace bodices with long, floating chiffon skirts. Maureen was in lavender, and Jennifer's gown was a peach colour. She gazed into the mirror as it was pinned on her and she felt at that moment as if she were a princess.

"You look really pretty," admired Kathy.

Through the glass Jennifer glanced at her. How would she behave if she were placed in Kathy's position? she asked herself. She would work just as eagerly and as well, came the answer. Jennifer was suddenly stricken with guilt. It was her own insecurity that had made her resentful of Kathy, yet this situation must have been just as hard on her.

"Thank you," Jennifer said.

Returning downstairs, the girls ran into Danièlle. Jennifer was delighted. For weeks she hadn't seen her friend who was now leading a very busy life as a professional dancer. Jennifer sensed a change in her although she wasn't sure what it was. She felt proud that Danièlle greeted her so warmly in front of Maureen and Kathy.

"Well, how did your first rehearsal go?" Danièlle asked.

"Fine," answered Jennifer enthusiastically.

"And they have gorgeous costumes," added Kathy.

"I know," Danièlle laughed. "All the designs for this ballet are incredibly beautiful. Wait till you see mine. I'm one of the courtiers in the ballroom scene."

"Oh! Then we'll be on stage at the same time," Jennifer blurted out.

"Yes," replied Danièlle. She squeezed her friend's hand. "We'll be able to give each other courage. I'll really need it. The variations I have to dance are dreadfully complicated. Oh!" she checked her watch. "I must go. I'm late for a *Swan Lake* rehearsal. Wish me luck. It's with the artistic directors. See you soon." And she took off down one of the mysterious corridors.

Jennifer watched her go. Danièlle looked tired and happy, but nervous. She remembered that Miss Collins had said that the first season in a professional company was a very strenuous one.

The girls would have loved to lurk backstage longer but it was already six o'clock. Jennifer was due back for dinner. At the subway, she said goodbye to Maureen and Kathy and walked up the street to the Student House.

There were very few children staying there now, for almost everyone had gone home for Christmas. Jennifer preferred it this way. There was a peace about the place instead of the usual hysteria. The school building had become even more beautiful at this time of year. Snow-flakes lodged on the old walls and twinkling Christmas lights made mysteries of all the shadows in the stone. Even Mrs. Peers had calmed down although she claimed she was still "run off her feet" with her duties. She must have been kept fairly busy, for the occasion never arose for her to free her hair from the steel clips. Jennifer began to wonder if Mrs. Peers wound her pin curls daily or whether, in fact, her head had been in that state for years.

That night Jennifer felt lonely in her attic room. She listened to rustles and squeaks that she had never heard before. Abashed that she had looked forward to Suzanne and Emily being gone, Jennifer now couldn't take her mind off her roommates. She thought of Mrs. Stock, and chuckled inwardly. Emily would have a warm and cheery Christmas in Edmonton. She hoped that Suzanne was happy at last, now that she was home again.

Jennifer gazed for a long time at the silver framed photo beside her bed. There they all were: Mum and Dad, Jim and Sue, and Jennifer, smiling outside their yellow brick house shortly after coming to Canada. That was two years ago. So much had happened since. Jennifer wondered if the rest of her family were as changed as she was.

Her feet ached and the left ankle was feeling sore and tender. Rubbing it, she almost welcomed this reminder of her exciting day. Now, how did it begin? she asked herself. She wanted to preserve and store every detail in her mind forever. Backstage had been another world. Jennifer had sensed a difference the instant she walked in the stage door. Only very special people entered there, and now she was almost one of them.

Part III

Jennifer sat pouting at the lunch table. She was there against her will, for today the last thing she was interested in was food. Besides, her stomach was misbehaving in an alarming manner. For the past week it had felt just as when she had crossed the ocean – all topsy-turvy. Today it was even worse, as if inside-out and upside-down. Jennifer couldn't eat, yet Mrs. Peers would not excuse her from the table.

"You've got stage fright. Stage fright," she announced with finality. "Now there's no need to be nervous!"

Jennifer didn't want to admit, even to herself, that the woman might be right, although it was true that today was the twentieth of December and tonight she would be performing on stage in *Cinderella*.

Jennifer groaned at her plate piled high with meat

and vegetables. Mrs. Peers had served bigger portions than usual to the performing students.

"Eat up! Eat up! You're going to need all your strength for tonight," she kept saying. Jennifer remained still, and each time Mrs. Peers said "tonight" in that meaningful way, her insides shivered.

Just when Jennifer grew impatient of inventing excuses and decided she could not stay another minute, Mrs. Peers came out of the kitchen.

"Perhaps this will settle those butterflies down," she said with a mysterious look on her face, and she placed in front of Jennifer a dish of maple ice cream swimming in hot fudge sauce. Jennifer's appetite suddenly perked up. It had been a long time since she'd eaten her favourite dessert and she polished her spoon clean after every bite.

As soon as she was finished she excused herself from the table and raced upstairs to peek inside her bursting yellow bag. She wanted to check its contents just one more time. She emptied the bag completely so that she could tick off each item on her list: ballet shoes, pink tights, Kleenex, hair brush, mirror, soap and towel. Oh, yes, she needed a comb too. Then Jennifer remembered Danièlle's warning that it was always cold backstage, so she ran and got her dressing gown to wear between changes. Making as small a bundle as she could, she placed it among the other items.

Make-up had been number one on Jennifer's list but she didn't have any to pack. She had already confessed to Danièlle that she was worried about what to buy. Her friend offered to provide both Jennifer and Maureen with whatever they needed, for she had just invested in a whole new make-up kit.

"You won't be expected to wear very much," Danièlle said. "A little lipstick and rouge will do you fine."

Jennifer had been a trifle disappointed although she tried not to show it. She had pictured herself fluttering long, silken eyelashes over heavily shadowed eyes.

Jennifer was in the midst of reorganizing when she heard Mrs. Peers call from downstairs.

"Hurry up, Jennifer, it's time to go!"

Again her stomach started to rollercoast and her hands shook as she quickly restuffed her things into the yellow bag. She was halfway down the stairs when she remembered her coat. Back up to the room she ran.

Dressed in her warm duffle coat and black rubber boots, Jennifer was finally ready. Mrs. Peers was waiting for her in the front hall.

"After all your mooning about these performances, here you're almost late!" she muttered as she checked Jennifer over. She solemnly handed Jennifer a brown paper bag. "There's apples and oranges," she said. "You won't have time to eat dinner so you can nibble on these backstage."

"Thank you," murmured Jennifer. Now she remembered something Danièlle had said: "Professional dancers don't eat their dinner until after the show because it's impossible to dance with a heavy meal in the stomach."

"Well, good luck, then," said Mrs. Peers, as Jennifer stood awkwardly in the doorway. "Do me proud now."

Jennifer blinked at the woman. Did Mrs. Peers have a tear in her eye?

142

"Off you go," she commanded, giving Jennifer a hearty slap on her behind. "I'll pick you up at eleven-thirty tonight." Her voice betrayed no emotion, yet as Jennifer glanced back from the street, there stood Mrs. Peers energetically waving at her.

On the subway Jennifer could not keep her mind still. It danced over every inch of the choreography. What if I miss my entrance? the thought suddenly popped into her head. Then she remembered Danièlle's stories of performers who became so nervous that they blanked when they stepped out on stage. She fidgeted in her seat and her ankle sent out a little jab just to remind her that she had it to worry about as well.

As the train sped on, Jennifer looked at the people sitting around her, examining their bored and tired faces. She had an urge to yell out her delicious secret to them – where she was going, what she was about to do. She tried to guess which of the passengers had ever seen a performance. She often forgot that there was a world outside hers where some people didn't know what ballet was about.

Jennifer's dreamy gaze shifted to the open doors and with a start she realized that she was staring at her stop. Hastily grabbing her yellow bag she nipped through the narrowing gap. It was too late when Jennifer remembered the brown paper bag with its apples and oranges, and she watched the train disappear down the black tunnel. Oh well, the last thing she was interested in today was food.

Chapter Eighteen

*J*ennifer arrived at the stage door at seven minutes after four to find Maureen waiting for her.

"I was getting worried that you weren't coming," she said. Jennifer noticed a nervous look in her eyes.

"Where's Kathy?" she asked Maureen.

"They told her she was no longer needed now that your foot is better, but Miss Collins got her a ticket for tonight."

The two girls handed the doorman the special passes they had been given by Miss Collins. He didn't bother to check them.

"You're to change in dressing room 950," he said, and seeing Jennifer and Maureen hesitate in the doorway, he left the glass entrance booth and led them inside to the

144

steep spiral staircase. "Climb right to the top, little ones. You've a long way to go."

By the time they arrived at the ninth floor, Jennifer and Maureen were worn out. Room 950 had a piece of paper stuck on the outside on which was printed: SCHOOL STUDENTS (GIRLS). They knocked and waited. There was no answer. Jennifer knocked again, then cautiously inched the door open. There was no one inside the tiny room and the girls entered, flopping down exhausted on the rickety wooden chairs. The room was freezing cold although a radiator clinked and rattled in the corner. Beside it was a sink with one tap from which water escaped in a hissing stream. Jennifer reached to warm her hands along the row of glowing light bulbs. They framed a dirty mirror tacked up on the wall with a taped crack splitting it in half.

Jennifer started to unpack; she wanted to settle in so she could feel she really belonged here. She pulled her things out of the yellow bag and very neatly arranged them on the wooden counter in front of her. Luckily she had remembered to bring her own mirror and she now polished it clean. Maureen soon followed her example and the two girls were silent while they organized themselves in their new surroundings.

"What do you think we should do next?" Maureen asked minutes later, sticking her head out into the deserted hallway.

"Maybe we should change into our practise clothes for class," Jennifer suggested. She had thought that on this special day they might be excused from their ballet exercises, but Danièlle had been horrified when Jennifer mentioned this to her.

"On performance days class is absolutely essential to a dancer," she cried. "No ballerina would dream of setting foot on the stage without first doing all her exercises. For *Cinderella* I shall take a class at noon, a warm-up and rehearsals at five, and then probably a short barre five minutes before I go on stage. Watch the other professionals. You'll see."

Jennifer felt ashamed for asking, although she still wondered how the dancers weren't exhausted by the time they had to perform.

"Stamina," Danièlle had said. "It's a special strength that you develop from all the years of training."

Dressed in their pink tights and black leotards, the two girls finally decided to venture downstairs again. Arriving on the main floor they followed a narrow corridor to where a piano was playing. Through the door of a large ballet studio they could see that rehearsals were in progress. The professional dancers were clothed in every conceivable colour and they wore many layers of woollen garments. They looked tired and their faces were covered with sweat.

Jennifer recognized the ballet mistress who had taught her the steps of the ballet. She was busy counting out the beat of the music to a group of dancers. "One and two, three and four," she kept repeating. "Don't forget the plié is on one and the arabesque is on two. You must be *exactly* on the beat," she stressed.

Danièlle was there, wearing a white top and red sweat

pants. She signalled to the two girls to wait and they settled themselves on the floor in a corner. They were watching, fascinated, when they heard a voice from above. It was Madame Rose. Jennifer and Maureen jumped up quickly. They hadn't expected to see their school principal here.

"Come with me, girls," she said. "I want to show you the stage while it's free. There's a lot to explain to you."

At last! Jennifer had been waiting for this! So far, all her rehearsals had been in a studio. She followed Madame Rose and Maureen down a long corridor until they came to a massive iron door. Painted on it was STAGE. Underneath in even larger print: NO ADMITTANCE. Madame Rose ignored this and gave the door a mighty push.

For a second Jennifer hesitated, but then she had to follow. The heavy door had slammed shut behind her and she could hardly see anything in the sudden dark. Blinking her eyes she finally made out the forms of Madame Rose and Maureen who were already far ahead of her. Madame Rose waited for Jennifer to catch up, then she indicated the rows of black velvet curtains.

"In theatre language these are called the wings, where you make your entrances and exits. And these are the lights that illuminate the stage area." She pointed to the giant metal contraptions standing in the spaces between the drapes. "You must be very careful not to knock them as you run on and off the stage. Now, follow me carefully."

The ground was covered with a network of knotted ropes and cables. Jennifer kept tripping as she tried to keep up with Madame Rose who gracefully manoeuvred around all the obstacles.

Suddenly Jennifer realized that she was being led onto the stage itself. Madame Rose had halted in the centre of an enormous rectangular area. Jennifer looked across to see a corresponding set of wings; behind her hung more black velvet curtains, in front stretched endless space. Maureen pointed to the edge of the stage along which was tacked a string of miniature lights. Madame Rose noticed her puzzled look.

"Those are much the same as Christmas tree lights," she said smiling, "and they are placed there so the dancers won't become dizzy and forget about the orchestra pit."

Both girls' eyes widened at this.

"How far does it go down there?" Maureen asked.

"Well, it must be quite a drop," laughed Madame Rose, "but don't worry, the lights are merely a precaution."

Tilting back her head, Madame Rose gestured directly above them. Following her gaze Jennifer made out the discs of more unused lights. Beyond them stretched blackness. There was no discernible ceiling.

"Those are called the *flies*," Madame Rose continued, "where the ropes and wires and pulleys are located to manipulate the sets and curtains. There are some members of the stage crew who work up there throughout the whole performance."

"Wow! How high does it go?" asked Jennifer.

"About thirty-five feet," answered Madame Rose. She was amused at her students' reaction to the vastness of the stage, but she was not surprised. Despite all her years in the theatre, she was still impressed by its immensity.

Filled with awe, Jennifer's eyes wandered beyond the footlights to the countless rows of empty seats rising all the way up to the top balcony. Was it possible that in a few hours there would be a live audience out there? "How many people will be coming tonight?" she asked softly.

"Well, we're sold out," Madame Rose sounded pleased, "and this theatre has two thousand eight hundred seats."

Jennifer gasped. With so many people watching, she'd better not make any mistakes! The stage had no walls, nor did it have the mirror to which she had grown accustomed to reassure her of the correctness of her movements. In class if Jennifer forgot an exercise she could always copy her fellow students through the glass; and when she faltered she was allowed to try again. Standing on the barren stage in the half light, she felt strangely small and insignificant.

"Well, girls, the company dancers will soon be wanting to use the stage. So let's begin our rehearsal," said Madame Rose. "You enter from the curved staircase on stage right and descend very slowly, holding Cinderella's silver train. Your feet must be pointed and your chin raised. Watch." Madame Rose seemed to float down the stairs. "Now, can you remember what happens next?"

Jennifer, surprised to see Maureen frown and look unsure, nodded eagerly and demonstrated the lilting dance the ballet mistress had shown them.

"Not bad," said Madame Rose when she finished. "But try once again with Maureen. I want you both to concentrate on moving exactly together. This is very important."

Jennifer repeated the entrance, this time watching Maureen out of the corner of her eye. She didn't enjoy having to conform, but she reminded herself that this was very much a part of ballet discipline.

"Let's go on to your Midnight Dance of Fright," said Madame Rose. She made them repeat this passage many times until they were dancing the steps to her satisfaction. "Be sure you exit by the middle stage-left wing," she said. "There's a sixty-second set change right after the twelfth stroke."

Jennifer absorbed every one of Madame Rose's words and gestures. She had never actually worked with her principal before, and she hoped she was making a good impression. Madame Rose was turning out to be far less awesome than she appeared. From the start her presence had inspired Jennifer to dance better. Everyone knew what a great ballerina she had been before she became a teacher. Her photograph was in all the important ballet books and Jennifer had even found one picture of her as Cinderella! It had been taken many years ago when Madame Rose was young and beautiful.

The dimly lit stage gradually became cluttered with company dancers practising different parts of the ballet and going over their individual problems. One man and woman nearly collided several times with Maureen and Jennifer, but Madame Rose didn't seem to mind. For these particular dancers she often stopped rehearsal and stepped aside, allowing them to complete a lift. They would perform their steps over and over again, afterwards discussing each attempt in detail. Jennifer began to wonder: could they possibly be Cinderella and the Prince?

It was frustrating not to know the rest of the cast and she had scarcely concealed her surprise and dismay when her rehearsals were never with the performing company. Danièlle explained one day that extras were fitted into the production at the last minute. It was the same on tour, with different children performing in every new city.

Maureen must have had the same thoughts as Jennifer. "Excuse me, Madame Rose, but how will we know who Cinderella is?" she asked.

"How silly of me," their principal said. "I just assumed you knew, since we've been working right beside her."

She waited for the couple to complete one of their beautiful lifts. "They're going over the pas de deux right now," she explained. Jennifer heard the pride in Madame Rose's voice and she wondered if at one time these dancers had also been her students. As she watched, she marvelled at the seeming effortlessness of their take-offs and landings.

"That was better!" the girl said to her partner as she came down from an overhead swoop. "Does it help you when I arch my back like that? I think we've found the secret!"

Madame Rose interrupted. "Grace, I would like you to meet Maureen and Jennifer. They'll be your pages in the ballroom scene tonight. Girls, this is Cinderella."

"And her handsome Prince," added the man, grinning.

Jennifer giggled. He was good-looking.

The girl named Grace turned to Jennifer. "Hi, you're Danièlle's friend, aren't you?"

Jennifer nodded, proud that she knew, hoping Madame Rose had heard.

"I'll be dressed in silver tonight for the ballroom scene," she continued, "and you two must be sure to help me by carrying my long train. I'd have difficulty getting down the stairs without you. You won't forget, will you?"

The girls shook their heads. How could we? Jennifer thought.

"You don't have to do anything for me except enjoy the show," the Prince joined in. He smiled at the girls' upturned faces. "How do you feel?"

"Scared," Maureen replied, while Jennifer continued with her nodding. To the girls' surprise, Madame Rose laughed at this along with the two professional dancers.

"We're scared too," Grace said. "Only none of us ever likes to admit it. Don't worry, it's perfectly normal."

Madame Rose checked her watch. "Oh my goodness!" she exclaimed. "It's six o'clock. We'd better get you two girls made up before your ballet class. Quick, follow me."

As they hurried off, Jennifer looked back over her shoulder. The Prince waved. "Good luck," he called. But Cinderella had already started to practise again.

Madame Rose paused in the wings. "I have an important meeting now," she said, looking again at her watch.

"So the best thing for you girls is to go up to the Corps de Ballet dressing room on the fourth floor. That's where most of the dancers get changed." She turned to Jennifer. "And that's where you'll find your friend Dan-ièlle. Do you think she'd mind helping you girls with make-up?"

"Oh no," answered Jennifer, hoping she was right.

Madame Rose led them out the iron door to the circular staircase. As the girls started to climb, she called up after them, "Class will be in Studio C at six-forty-five sharp."

"Well!" said Jennifer between breaths as they plodded. "Who would have thought that we'd have so much to do on the day of the performance!"

"Mmmm," answered Maureen, preoccupied. She had been very quiet all day and Jennifer wondered what was the matter. "Do you remember the new step that Madame Rose showed us?" she suddenly asked. Jennifer was struck by the panic in Maureen's voice. This was the girl who never seemed to find anything difficult.

"I think so," Jennifer answered, and ashamed of her superior feelings she added reassuringly, "Let's go over all our steps together later."

The door to the women's Corps de Ballet dressing room was open. The girls peeped inside to see a room about five times the size of theirs on the ninth floor. There were rows of mirrors framed in lights and in front of each sat a young woman painting on the face of a dancer. All was in colourful confusion, with ballet slippers, practise clothes and Kleenex boxes littering the floor. Blue jeans and sweaters hung on the racks amid costumes of gold and silver. Unnoticed, Jennifer and Maureen picked their way down the rows until they spotted Danièlle. She was seated at the far end and was not involved in the gossip and laughter around her. The two girls watched as she back-combed her copper-coloured hair into the classical style.

"I didn't think you'd have to do your own hair as well!" exclaimed Maureen.

"Hi, oh yes," Danièlle answered without taking her eyes away from the mirror. "Ballerinas do everything for themselves – make-up, hair, sewing ribbons on pointe shoes, everything. Help yourself, " she added, pointing to the various pots and brushes on the counter.

Maureen hesitated, looking at the many rouges and lipsticks, but Jennifer jumped at the chance. Ever since her visit to Smith's Theatrical Supplies she had dreamed of the time when she would use stage make-up herself. She lifted a jar of creamy rouge and dabbing her fingers in, she spread it on her cheeks. She looked up at herself in the mirror to admire, then gasped at what she'd done. Instead of the warm glow that Danièlle had, Jennifer's face gleamed like a circus clown's.

Danièlle took one look at her flaming cheeks and laughed. "You know, I sometimes forget how young you really are," she said. "I'll help you as soon as I'm sure this headdress is pinned securely in place."

By the time Danièlle finished with Jennifer and Maureen, they looked the way fairy attendants must look. She had painted a soft glow on their cheeks and lips and had tied their hair into identical buns.

Staring into the mirror, Jennifer felt both pretty

and professional. What made her especially happy were the peach satin ribbons which were wound around her hair into delicate bows at the back. Danièlle made the two girls stand next to each other in front of the mirror and she stepped back to admire her work.

"You look super," she said and she gave them each a hug. She reached for some pointe shoes. "I must go. It's time for the company warm-up. I'll see you on stage later."

Class for the students was held separately in Studio C. Jennifer and Maureen were five minutes late and they could hear the music as they hurried into the room. Madame Rose was taking class too. This was quite a day of new experiences! She nodded, unruffled at the girls' apologies, and gestured to a place at the barre.

"We'll do a forty-five-minute barre," she said, "to make sure your muscles are good and warm for the performance."

Jennifer worked diligently. She didn't need to remind herself that this was the most important ballet class she had ever taken.

Chapter Nineteen

By eight o'clock that evening the two exhausted girls were back in their room on the ninth floor. Jennifer's foot was throbbing from all the extra demands she had made on it that day. What a relief to be sitting down, and she propped her weary legs up on the counter. Beside her, Maureen munched busily on an apple and then dissected an orange. But Jennifer just pondered her altered reflection in the mirror. She loved the way Danièlle had done her hair. Would she ever be able to fix it that way herself? It seemed doubtful. Yet the Jennifer that stared at her from the glass seemed to say that she could do anything.

What a full day this had been, and it was only in preparation of something that hadn't even happened yet! Over the loudspeaker Jennifer could hear a few musicians already in the pit. She picked out the piccolo and the flute as they tuned up together, and she recognized fragments from the *Cinderella* score.

Suddenly a man's voice broke in. "Half an hour, please. Thirty minutes to curtain. Half an hour, please."

The girls sat up, their eyes meeting instantly in the mirror. Jennifer could feel her insides stirring with excitement. And miraculously her fatigue slipped away.

There was a tap at the door. "Come in," both girls called at once.

In marched the wardrobe mistress with the peach and lavender costumes over her arm. "Well, young ladies, it's time to get dressed," she announced.

Jennifer, who had been a trifle worried that the costumes wouldn't appear, leapt to her feet. All day she'd been looking forward to this moment.

As Jennifer's back hooks were being fastened, she watched her transformation in the cracked mirror. The peach gown fit her perfectly and its soft chiffon skirt floated after her as she swayed from side to side. The bodice glinted with tiny diamonds and pearls that had been stitched into the lace. Her glowing face and ribboned hair completed the picture. Now she saw a Jennifer looking like the photos of the ballerinas she had admired in books. That's me! she told herself. If only my family could see me now. Jim and Sue would never recognize me as their little sister!

"You look as pretty as a picture," said the wardrobe mistress, as though reading her mind.

Jennifer blushed, but as she waited for Maureen to get dressed her eyes kept flickering back to the mirror. It

was impossible to keep still; too many feelings were racing inside her. She wanted to dance!

At last Maureen was ready, and two girls with shining eyes descended the winding staircase to the main floor.

Backstage was bustling with activity. The halls, hushed an hour ago, were now filled with people frantically running up and down, intent upon their business. As they hurried by, the stage crew and dancers never noticed Maureen and Jennifer standing there. It was as though they wore blinkers. At the ends of the corridors stood groups of important-looking people consuming coffee and involved in earnest discussions. With their eyes they communicated tension and excitement.

Every few minutes a dressing-room door would open and a head would poke out yelling, "Dresser!" At this signal some frightened lady carrying a costume would scurry in and the door would slam shut. Twice, the worried-looking ballet mistress running from room to room with her notebook of corrections was bumped by enormous baskets of flowers which were being delivered. No matter where they went, Jennifer and Maureen managed to be in somebody's way. At one point Jennifer collided with a large man who was pacing up and down, humming and waving a stick.

"Oh, excuse me," she apologized, horrified when she realized she had stepped on the toes of the conductor.

"Never mind, little one," he said in a warm booming voice, "a lot of that goes on around here." But he rubbed his foot when he thought Jennifer was no longer looking.

The two girls finally managed to slip inside the iron door to the stage, but this turned out to be the busiest place of all. They had intruded upon chaos! Hammers pounded. Stage hands hollered. Massive pieces of scenery were hauled about with great swiftness. Dancers argued with the stage manager for tiny portions of the stage. Dizzying lights blinked in every direction.

On the other side of the curtain there was even more noise. In the orchestra pit a growing number of musicians droned on their instruments, and the audience accompanied the din with chatter and laughter as they filled their seats.

"Fifteen minutes, please. Fifteen minutes to curtain," bellowed the red-faced stage manager. No one appeared to hear him, yet the tension mounted.

Bewildered and confused, Jennifer was greatly relieved when Danièlle suddenly appeared. He gown rustled in a wonderful way and her sleek chestnut hair was adorned with a headdress of pearls. From under elongated lashes, her grey eyes flashed with extra sparkle. For a second Jennifer felt intense shyness seeing the radiance of her friend. Then she remembered that she and Maureen were also a part of the magic.

"You both look lovely!" Danièlle exclaimed as she took their hands. "Guess what? I've found the perfect place for you two. I've obtained permission from the directors for you to watch the first act from the front wing," she announced triumphantly.

Jennifer stood quite still. She didn't dare let on that she had already assumed they would watch.

"You're really lucky," Danièlle added. "They don't

usually allow non-company members to sit in the wings, but I assured them you'd make yourselves invisible."

Danièlle guided them through the tumult to the stage-right wing. She had a few words with one of the stage hands who finally, with a shrug of his shoulders, placed two stools for them in a tiny nook in the shadows. It was true that you could hardly even notice Jennifer and Maureen when they were seated in the corner, but they could see the entire stage and beyond to the wings on the other side.

"On stage. On stage, please," announced the stage manager. "Curtain goes up in two minutes. Orchestra to the pit, please. On stage."

"I'll leave you now," said Danièlle, "and I'll be back at the end of the first act."

Suddenly all the lights went out and a deep hush enveloped everything. This was the moment of expectancy that Jennifer remembered and cherished from the ballet performance in London. She could see nothing in the dark around her but she sensed the audience fall silent with rapt suspense. At a cue from the conductor the first full chords from the strings signalled the commencement of the performance.

Behind the curtain the stage manager whispered urgently. "Places, please. On stage, please. Going up in thirty seconds."

From the wings and above, lights gradually focussed their tinted beams and Jennifer and Maureen observed what the audience would never see. Cinderella, instead of scrubbing and sweeping, was trying last-minute pirouettes. The Ugly Sisters, while peeling off layers of woollen socks, were in hurried consultation. Then, five times they practised tumbling in through an archway together. The Stepmother simply paced about the stage, deep in thought, and every once in a while gave her nose a hearty blow. It seemed they all ignored the muffled music and the red-faced man in the wings who was signalling madly to them. Then, with daring casualness, the Ugly ones wandered off the stage and Cinderella dropped to her knees in front of the fireplace. She froze into position. The pieces of the opening scene suddenly fit. The curtain was rising.

Chapter Twenty

She's quite a dancer, isn't she?" whispered Maureen, and Jennifer nodded, never taking her eyes off Cinderella. Her opening solo was filled with complicated combinations of pirouettes, and the ballerina mastered them all with unbelievable ease. Her lyrical style and floating arms never gave away the difficulty of the steps she was dancing, but from where they were sitting Jennifer could see the concentration in her eyes and hear her breath quickening.

The Ugly Sisters' entrance was hilarious. They literally tumbled onto the stage in a series of whirling somersaults and the audience roared in appreciation. They bickered with each other while mercilessly hammering the toes of their pointe shoes into the resonant floor. Their eyeballs roved and their lips pouted. With their whole bodies they mocked themselves. Yet, at the same time, they were dancing with unquestionable skill, for it was almost impossible to follow their intricate and nimble footwork. Suddenly they wheeled around to face Jennifer, and to her astonishment they marched right to where she and Maureen were sitting. The minute they stepped into the shadowy wing, their animated faces darkened with fatigue. They both puffed and panted as if they had been running in a race. They massaged their legs and blotted their sweaty faces.

"Water!" gasped the smaller dancer when she finally found breath to speak. One of the company members handed her a rubber bottle and she squirted drops into her mouth.

"How was it?" the taller sister whispered to anyone around. "Wasn't the music too fast? How did our variation look?" Then, without waiting for an answer, she turned, took a deep breath and lunged back out under the lights. Instantly her lips stretched into a comic grin.

The story was unfolding vividly. So often Jennifer would lose herself in the action, chuckling and reacting along with the audience and having to restrain herself from clapping. But there was even more to see from her little nook, making Jennifer feel wonderfully invisible. During a fighting scene, the raging Stepmother skidded and fell in the middle of a *posé* turn. She was up instantly with an elaborate flourish of her arms so that no one in the audience would ever have known that anything unusual had happened.

"Are you all right?" one of the sisters whispered to her when their backs were turned to the public.

"Fine," murmured the Stepmother as she continued with her darting, swooping dance.

In the front wing all the way across from where Jennifer and Maureen were sitting, the stage manager was stationed at his desk. He had earphones on his head and a microphone in his hand. He alternated watching the action on stage with following the musical score while he called out the various cues to the lighting men and the stage crew in the flies. Behind him and in the other wings hovered dancers who would perform later in the evening. Some of them were dressed in their costumes, while others had added layers to their wollen tights. They all seemed unable to keep still, their knees bending and their feet pointing as they watched their colleagues on the stage.

What delighted Jennifer most was how many ballet steps she recognized. Some of them she could even do! Jennifer's ballet studies had given her new knowledge and a deeper appreciation of what she was observing. The dancers were pirouetting with precision and speed. They were leaping with stretched legs and pointed toes; they were making her laugh and cry; they were dancing – superbly!

* * *

The first act came to an end and the heavy curtain lowered, muffling the audience's enthusiastic response. When Danièlle came to collect her two wards, she found them applauding and discussing the dancing.

"Wasn't it wonderful!" they both blurted out as soon as they saw Danièlle.

She laughed. "Yes, they're really 'on' tonight."

Jennifer knew what that meant. There were "on" days and "off" days for all dancers whether they were beginning or experienced. You could master a step one day and be utterly unable to do it the next. That was what was so frustrating about working with your own body – it could be so unpredictable. "We dancers spend our whole lives searching for the secret of total control, and yet in the end we all hope for luck when we step out on the stage," Danièlle had said.

"How long will intermission last?" asked Maureen.

"About twenty minutes," Danièlle answered.

"And then it'll be our turn to appear on stage?" Jennifer questioned, although she already knew the answer.

"Why, yes," said Danièlle. "They're already hanging the sets for the ballroom scene."

Maureen's face had gone white and she looked as if she were about to cry. "I'm not sure I'm ready," she confessed. "In fact, I feel sick."

"Come on," said Jennifer, "we'll go over everything from beginning to end, then you'll feel better." She felt very sorry for Maureen, more so because she'd envied her so much in the past. She too had had the jitters. They had plagued her all week, but now she was somehow drained of all her worries.

The sets were changed and when the all-clear signal was given the dancers crowding the wings rushed out to do their last-minute practising. Jennifer and Maureen followed Danièlle. For one moment Jennifer faced the lowered curtain, thinking of the two thousand eight hundred people waiting on the other side. Then she turned to Maureen and started to review their choreography. Some steps they repeated over and over again, but all around them professional dancers were doing exactly the same thing. Cinderella came up to them and pointed out the staircase where they would make their entrance. She had changed from her rags into a beautiful gown of spun silver silk that shimmered under the lights.

"Now don't forget, I need you to hold my train," she reminded them. "It's really very long."

Immediately picking it up, Jennifer marvelled at the delicacy of the material. It felt as though it had been fashioned by magic hands and then she remembered she was supposed to be a fairy attendant.

It was hard keeping up with Cinderella as she darted about the stage talking with various dancers and consulting the conductor about a tempo. The two girls had to keep their wits about them, for she moved swiftly and changed her direction without warning. The next thing they knew, she was heading out of the iron door and rushing back to the dressing room.

"I've forgotten my necklace," she called to the stage manager.

The girls scurried after her, clutching onto her dress as hard as they could. Feeling the tugs, she looked around in surprise. Seeing them still hanging onto her, she burst into laugher.

"Oh no, not now," she exclaimed. "You don't have to worry about me now. Only when the curtain goes up and we enter on stage."

The girls nodded sheepishly.

"You poor things," she chuckled. "I've led you a

merry dance. Well, now I know you'll be able to handle that staircase." And she laughed again.

Cinderella opened the door to her dressing room. It had a star on it. "Would you like to come in?" she asked, seeing Jennifer peek inside.

The girls nodded again.

"Well," said Cinderella, "we only have a minute, but you're welcome to take a quick look. You can come after the show for a longer visit."

They were in and out in a flash, but not so fast that Jennifer didn't notice the difference between the star's dressing room and Danièlle's in the Corps de Ballet. She saw a flurry of costumes and flowers and ballet shoes, a couch, a gleaming mirror, a counter covered with open make-up jars and brushes.

"On stage, please. On stage," the call came over the loudspeaker as Cinderella rummaged through a jewel box for her necklace.

"Let's go," she said as she fastened it around her neck. "I must practise a step from my solo before the curtain goes up or it'll be bad luck." She unhooked her train as they headed back to the stage area. "Here, if you girls hold this for me and wait by the bottom of the staircase, it will be a great help. Chuckers to you two," Cinderella added. "That's a special wish from the ballet world that will never fail you."

Jennifer and Maureen looked at each other. "Chuckers," they repeated as they carried the gossamer cloak back to the stage.

Chapter Twenty-One

When the curtain rose on the second act the audience burst into applause. The sets for the ballroom scene were magnificent! Three massive chandeliers were suspended from the flies, their crystal drops sparkling under the lights. Drapes of antique gold were swathed in graceful arches and the painted pillars looked like columns of marble. The courtiers at the palace ball were dressed in robes of gold and silver that were lavishly adorned with jewels. They drew ever-changing patterns as they danced a majestic gavotte.

Waiting offstage by the staircase, Jennifer peeked through a crack in the scenery and listened to the music for her cue. Beside her stood Maureen clinging to her portion of the cloak.

"It won't be long now," whispered Cinderella, and Jennifer turned to see her bobbing up and down, then jogging from one foot to the other. She had a deeply concentrated look on her face as she followed the action on the stage. Jennifer suspected the ballerina was experiencing the same pangs and flutters as she and Maureen were. She reground her satin pointe shoes into the resin box and smoothed her silver dress for what must have been the fiftieth time.

Then Jennifer heard the change in the music which suggested the arrival of the beautiful princess. Cinderella took her place and the two girls mounted the rickety ramp behind their mistress. They could barely see each other in the shadows and they hardly dared breathe as they listened for their notes of introduction. Three pairs of hands and legs were shaking.

"Ready?" Cinderella whispered over her shoulder. "Chuckers, you two. Here we go."

Blazing lights on a floodlit stage blinded Jennifer as she stepped out from the shelter of the wing. Blinking, her eyes gradually focussed on the Prince who stared up to where she stood beside Cinderella. The wonder in his face made her really believe she was a fairy princess. She was no longer ordinary Jennifer Allen. She felt that she was beautiful and she beamed at the other dancers who were all conspirators in her dream.

Regally she descended the staircase, taking care to catch the tip of Cinderella's floating train. The strings in the orchestra sang with a mystery Jennifer had not noticed before, and looking beyond the string of twinkling, tiny lights she could make out the top half of the conductor. He was looking up at the stage while waving his stick to the musicians below.

On cue, Jennifer and Maureen retreated to the side of the ballroom, seating themselves at the foot of a carved throne. Jennifer watched Cinderella dancing with the Prince, and her heart soared. This was the place she had always sought, where imaginings were real and where she could take part.

The sound of applause startled Jennifer. She had forgotten entirely about the audience. She concentrated her gaze into the blackness which concealed them. Now she could feel their presence – and their power. The thought of all those people did not terrify her. It somehow intensified her belief in the magic of the moment.

Jennifer didn't know that Dr. Sing was there as he said he might be, nor did the young doctor know that the excited people sitting beside him were from Sault Ste. Marie. Jennifer's family had disappointed her by a seeming lack of interest in the upcoming Christmas performance, while all along they were planning their surprise.

Times of joy move swiftly and Jennifer shared Cinderella's dismay when the first midnight gong shattered the melodic calm. Giving Maureen a nudge, she leapt up to the opening position of their choreographed Dance of Fright. *One! Two! Three!* With such prompting, Jennifer had no trouble remembering her steps. She pointed her fingers and with scampering feet she circled the stage. *Four! Five!* On her face she wore an expression of fear. And this was not pretend; she was possessed by the story of her dance. *Six! Seven! Eight!* Deep blue lights flashed in concert with the clock's discordant chimes. The stage had become a bewitched and stormy place.

Nine! Ten! Eleven! Jennifer whirled to the right and to the left, her arms urging Cinderella to leave. *Twelve!* Jennifer tore into the middle left wing on the final booming stroke.

She stood in the shadows, panting, stunned, excited and confused. Whatever had happened on that stage had been indescribable. Jennifer knew that she would never be the same again. She had discovered her dream.

In a daze she watched as the ballroom disintegrated. The stage hands were whisking away the sets and mounting the next scene in a blackout of sixty seconds.

Had she done the steps correctly? Would Madame Rose be pleased? In her intoxicated state, Jennifer had only fragmented images of the performance in her mind. Hours would be spent piecing them together, and years would be dedicated to tomorrow's dance.

Unwilling to take off her costume and make-up, she lingered with Maureen in the wings. A firm hand pressed on her shoulder startled her back to earth. It was the stage manager.

"You two come with me," he said.

Maureen and Jennifer exchanged frightened glances as they followed him to his desk. They were in for it now! He picked up two enormous bunches of flowers and handed one to each of them. "At the very end of the ballet, when the company is taking curtain calls, wait for my signal. I'll tell you when you should go," he whispered. Blank stares met his words, and throwing up his hands he said to Maureen, "You'll give your flowers to the Fairy Godmother, and you," he turned to Jennifer, "present yours to Cinderella."

The prickly stems of the deep wine roses told Jennifer that it was true. She inhaled their fragrance.

For the rest of the ballet Jennifer watched from the front wing at the stage manager's side. When the curtain lowered on the final scene, the audience came alive and the fervour of their applause brought smiles to every face backstage. Linking hands, the company dancers formed four rows of ten and they went repeatedly down to the edge of the stage, bowed to the audience, then backed up to where they had started.

"Now!" the stage manager whispered urgently. "Go!"

Once again Jennifer entered her chosen world. Cinderella, deep in a curtsy, did not see her coming and her face lit up as Jennifer shyly offered her the bouquet.

"Thank you," she said, gathering the roses in her arms. And as Jennifer turned towards the wings she added softly, "You danced beautifully. See you tomorrow night."